Her Royal Choice

Cassidy K. O'Connor

Prologue

"Addi, come see what we found."

Princess Addilyn pulled her bare feet out of the pond and ran to the three boys waiting for her. "What is it?"

Dorin brought something from around his back, it jumped out of his hands and straight towards her. A giant bullfrog landed at her feet as she screamed and stepped back.

"We found you a prince, all you have to do is kiss him." Beck laughed and nudged the frog with his toe sending it hopping away.

Noah, always the more thoughtful one rushed to apologize. "We're sorry, we didn't mean to scare you. Usually, these kinds of things don't gross you out."

Addi cleared her throat and smoothed her dress. "I wasn't afraid, I was startled by something flying at me." She gave each of them her most regal glare before spinning around and walking back to the pond where her shoes were sitting by the bank.

"Don't be mad Addi, we were just having fun." Beck plopped down next to her and grabbed his shoes.

"One day I'm going to be the Queen, and you boys won't be able to tease me anymore." As soon as the words were out of her mouth, all four grew silent.

This was their last day together for a long time. Addi had known all three boys since birth. They were the only other children she ever played with, they were her best friends. All four were turning thirteen soon, so the boys were being sent to a boarding school to finish their education.

Addi didn't understand why they couldn't stay and work with her tutors like they always had. She'd cried and begged her mother not to send them away, but she always got the same answer.

All young men are sent off for training to serve their country.

Addie didn't know what that meant, and no amount of begging changed the outcome. In a few hours, her only friends would be gone, and she would be alone.

Noah stood up and shook off the gloom first. "Come on guys, let's go see if Marta has any snacks in the kitchen."

All four ran for the castle, only slowing down when they broke through the trees and were back in sight of anyone that might be watching them. They took turns checking each other to make sure they were presentable. If Mrs. Parsons, their nanny, saw anything out of line or knew they had been running around barefoot like heathens she would have their heads.

Before they made it to the kitchen the door swung open, Mrs. Parsons stood there waiting for them. "Come along boys, the car is here to take you off to school."

The group stopped in their tracks, Addi's stomach rolled. "They aren't supposed to be leaving until after dinner." Her eyes filled with tears.

"None of that now, Princesses do not show such emotion." She waited for Addi to regain her composure before continuing on. "The Queen is waiting to say goodbye."

The sullen group dragged their feet down the halls. Addi could see servants were watching them, Marta was standing in the doorway to the kitchen wiping her eyes with her apron. Addi would never say it out loud, but Marta was more of a mother to all of them than their own.

She could understand the Queen not being overly loving and affectionate. Even the boy's parents never seemed to want to see them.

The boys lived in the castle and spent every minute with her. She overheard a few of the maids talking one time, they were discussing the foursome and who would win Addie. She didn't know what they were talking about, but they had spotted her through a crack in the door and ran off.

Mrs. Parsons cleared her throat getting Addi's attention, "You're falling behind, come along. You mustn't leave the Queen waiting."

All four lined up at the door to the throne room, clasped hands and walked in together. The Queen sat on the dais staring at them with one eyebrow quirked. The show of solidarity wasn't pre-arranged. No one faltered, they stopped in front of her and didn't let go of each other. Their bows and her curtsey were awkward because of it, but they didn't care.

"When you were selected as the Princesses companions, we had high standards for each of you. I'm pleased to say you have all done a fine job thus far. The next six years will be crucial to your development. Remember you were chosen over fifty other boys." Addi's eyes snapped to her mother's, she had no idea what the Queen was talking about. She glanced to the boy's faces, they didn't seem surprised by this announcement. "When we see you again, I expect there to be a clear front runner. I know you think you are friends now but remember you are competing as well."

All three boys bowed again and pulled a bewildered Addi out of the hall.

As the doors closed behind them they dropped hands, "What was that about? What's going on?" Addi searched each boy's face for answers.

The door opened again, Mrs. Parsons walked out quickly. "Say your goodbyes, let's go."

Dorin, the tallest of the three pulled her into a hug and whispered, "Be strong ducky, we'll be back before you know it."

Addi's throat was screaming in pain from the lump in her throat. Beck wrapped her in his arms and lifted her gently off the floor for a second, "Give Mrs. Parson's Hell for us, we'll see you soon."

Tears rolled down her face, her heart was breaking. Noah raised his arms, she ran into them. "We don't want to leave you, but we have to for a little while. I'm going to miss you. Every night I will make a wish on our star."

Mrs. Parson's cleared her throat, "Time to go."

Addie was surprised to see a tear roll down the older woman's cheek.

The foursome followed their nanny out the front of the castle, she put her arm around Addi's shoulders holding her firm. She must have been concerned Addi would try getting in the car with them.

"People are watching, look strong." Mrs. Parsons whispered to Addi.

She refrained from rolling her eyes and forced her royal training to kick in. She straightened her shoulders and waved goodbye to the three pieces of her heart as they rode away.

One

Six years, 5 months, 23 days later

Addi was sound asleep, completely unaware of the tears rolling down her cheeks. She was dreaming about a memory from when she was ten years old.

Queen Ellena was sitting next to her at breakfast. The boys sat across from her making faces at her when the Queen wasn't looking and trying to make her laugh. Ellena cleared her throat, clearly not oblivious to their game. "Addilyn, it's your birthday tomorrow. What would you like?"

Addi smiled wide, her new adult front teeth barely sticking through the gums. "Can I have a birthday party and we invite kids from the villages?"

Dorin chimed in. "Yeah, we can make it a carnival theme and play games."

Beck nodded excitedly. "Maybe Marta will make popcorn and corn dogs."

Noah, being the smallest of the three boys, had to lean forward to get their attention. "Can we find a clown to come too? They can paint our faces and make balloon animals."

Addi's eyes sparkled with excitement then quickly they dimmed with disappointment. It sounded like the perfect day...so of course, it wouldn't be allowed.

Her mother cleared her throat, everyone knew that meant to shut up and look at her. "A Princess doesn't need such frivolous entertainment." She leveled a stare at each boy before turning to Addi. "Marta will make you a special chocolate cake, and I'll send Niles to the village to buy you a nice necklace."

Addi was crushed, but there was nothing she could do. She nodded and finished her food in silence.

Later that night, Addi was hiding in the West tower when Noah burst through the door. "We have a surprise for you, come on."

She wasn't in the mood to play with them, but his excitement couldn't be ignored. She followed him downstairs, confused when he led her into the kitchen.

She gasped as she walked through the door.

"Surprise." The room was transformed, balloons and streamers were covering the walls and ceiling. Marta was standing by the counter holding a cake. Next to her was Niles wearing poorly done clown makeup. Most of the staff was there with small animals drawn on their cheeks.

Dorin, Beck, and Noah walked up with huge smiles on their faces.

Beck handed her a bowl of popcorn. "Happy Birthday Princess. We know you wanted more. This was the best we could do though."

Dorin pointed to the corner of the kitchen. "We didn't have any games to bring in, but Marta helped us set up bobbing for apples."

Noah interjected, "Make sure you do that before you get your face painted. Otherwise, you'll look like Niles."

The foursome giggled at the sad-looking clown.

Addi grabbed them into a hug, they moaned and groaned whenever she did that. "It's perfect, it's all I need."

A soft voice pulled her from the dream. "Addi wake up, are you all right?"

Addi blinked a few times, wiping the tears away. Addi glanced up at her maid, Shawna, embarrassed to be caught crying. "I'm fine, just a dream. Is everything okay?"

"Mrs. Parsons told me you have special guests arriving today, and I'm to spend extra time getting you ready." Shawna was brought in when Addi had turned sixteen. It was clear she was miserable without the boys nearby so the Queen, in one of her rare benevolent moments agreed to allow a girl similar to her age to come in and be her maid and companion. The Queen had interviewed quite a few girls before settling on Shawna.

Addi had overheard Mrs. Parsons talking with Marta, she said the girl was chosen because of her defects and therefore wouldn't be a distraction. This had angered Addi, the girl was beautiful in her opinion but because she had scarring across her face and one eye clouded over she was ignored by many. Addi let it go, she was too thrilled to have a friend she didn't care why she was chosen.

She forced away the melancholy feeling she always got when she thought of the boys and smiled at her best friend, "Do you know who these guests are?"

"I only know the staff was told to prepare three rooms." She leaned close and whispered into Addi's ear, "they prepared the three rooms in *this* hall."

Addi's mind raced, guests were always put in a separate wing away from the family residence. Why would these visitors get special treatment? "How very mysterious. Let's finish this torture and get downstairs, you have me curious now."

Twenty minutes later, Addi had been poked, prodded, and brushed until she shined. Usually, this much effort was only made when they were meeting with other royal families.

She made her way to the throne room and bowed to her mother before taking her seat at her side. Addi was set to turn 18 in three weeks, the

Queen had groomed her since birth for the day when she would rule. Addi had no idea when that would be, her mother was still young and healthy.

"Good morning, Addilyn, you look lovely." The Queen nodded to her before turning and whispering to one of her guards.

Addi's curiosity was peaked. She didn't see anyone special, and her mother wasn't giving away any clues as to who the visitors were.

The room was silent as the man made his way out of the room on an errand. A few seconds later, the doors opened, the guard returned with three men following closely behind.

The trio had no guards or staff of their own, so she assumed they weren't royalty. They made it to the dais and immediately knelt in front of the throne.

"You may rise, let us get a good look at you." In unison, the trio stood and stared straight at the Queen.

The back of Addi's neck was tingling, recognition slowly dawned on her. The three boys who had been taken from her all those years ago now stood before her as men. She studied each one's face, shocked at how much they had changed but at the same time were recognizable.

Her heart pounded in her chest, heat rushed to her face, her feet had pins and needles in them as she fought to stay composed. She wanted to run and jump into their arms, years of training had her sitting still as a stone.

"It would appear you have done well in your training while you were gone. I'm told you all received the highest marks in your classes, and you each have developed unique talents. Tomorrow will begin the process of elimination. Tonight, you will get settled in, and you may join us for dinner."

All three men nodded, turned on their heels, and strode from the room. Addi's stomach dropped, had they not recognized her? Were they not happy to see her?

"Addilyn, I can hear your mind racing from here." The Queen turned and waited for the barrage of questions she had to know was coming.

"Is that really them? Why are they here? Why didn't you tell me they were coming? What elimination process?" By the time the words had exploded out of her, she was slightly out of breath.

"Are you finished?" Her mother dispassionately stared at her.

Addi wanted to scream at her mother for always looking so composed while Addi felt like ants were crawling all over her body.

"Come to my chambers in one hour, we have much to discuss." Her mother stood and left without another word.

As soon as she was out of view, Addi jumped up and walked toward the door the boys had exited. She wanted to run, but there were still servants around, and she was expected to always act her part.

A moment of hesitation hit her as she reached to open the door. It had been six years; would they be the same? She took a deep breath and walked through. She was disappointed to see the hall was empty, she had hoped they would be waiting for her.

She had an hour before the audience with her mother and getting answers, so she decided to do what she always did when she was anxious. She turned and made her way toward the kitchens and to Marta. If Addi was lucky, she could get her to sneak sweets to her.

"Psst, ducky, in here." Addi turned and saw Dorin peeking out of a doorway. Relief swelled inside her, they did recognize her.

She glanced around to make sure no prying eyes were watching then made her way to the room. She slipped through the crack and closed it quietly behind her.

Addi turned and leaned back against the door for support. Her eyes were pointed down at the carpet, she slowly moved them upward until she reached their faces.

All three boys or she should say men were beaming at her. They started talking at the same time.

"Addi, it's so good to see you." Noah smiled.

"You've grown so much." Beck studied her from head to toe.

"Where's the gangly little girl who chased after us?" Dorin teased.

Addi chose to ignore Dorin's remark about her chasing them and the fact that he still called her that ridiculous nickname. When they were little, she was much smaller than them, so she was always awkwardly running trying to keep up. He said she reminded him of a baby duck chasing after it's mama.

She shrugged. "I can't believe you guys are here. Why did you ignore me before?" She didn't mean to ask. She was still a little hurt that they did.

"I couldn't ignore you if I tried," Noah's throaty declaration had her mouth go slightly dry. "But we were told to address the Queen only."

Beck reached forward, the back of his fingers rubbed along her cheek. "You aren't the little girl we left behind. My heart skipped a beat when I laid eyes on you."

Addi gulped loudly. Who are these sexy men and what happened to her goofball best friends?

"You didn't kiss any toads while we were away, did you?" Dorin had always been the leader of the group. It was odd to hear a hint of unsureness in his voice.

"As if Mrs. Parson's would let me near any toads. Once you left, I was thrown fully into preparing for the crown." She stepped forward and held her arms out. One by one they embraced her, the awkwardness easily slid away. It was replaced by nerves in her belly. Between the muscles in their arms and the smell of their skin, she was flushed and she didn't understand why. It dawned on her that she hadn't been near many guys her own age and she definitely had never kissed one. *Maybe this feeling was desire?*

Desperate for answers, she put aside her questions about her feelings, "Where have you been, tell me all about it." She sat in one of the overstuffed chairs and curled her legs under her as she did when they were young.

Each man stood still looking at her, they clearly knew they were going against protocol.

She rolled her eyes at them. "Come sit down, I want to talk. Please don't treat me like the Princess right now. Can't we be the fierce foursome again for a little while?"

Everyone chuckled at the nickname Marta had given them. They were hellions when they were young, they created masterful plans where two would distract while the other two snuck desserts from the kitchens.

Addi saw the indecision on their faces before they gave in and sat down. "We've been at school. Most of the time, we were with the other kids learning normal topics, but we also had private tutoring to prepare us for our return." Beck sat back in the chair as if that explained everything.

"Prepare for what? Are you to be my personal guards?" Addi chuckled at the idea.

"Perhaps we should talk again after you speak with your mother." Noah offered.

Addi held back her annoyance, they never had secrets from each other, and now she felt like there was a whole conspiracy about her that everyone knew about. "I see, well it just so happens I have to meet her now." She straightened her back, stood, and made her way to the door.

"Addi, don't be mad. It's not our place to tell you. Come back after you know everything and we'll tell you anything you want to know." Dorin's matter of fact tone didn't lessen her annoyance. She did the most royal thing she could think of, she didn't look back and strode out without a backward glance.

Two

Addi knocked on the large ornate double doors and waited. A few seconds later, the door was opened. Liza, her mother's maid stood back and let her in, she curtsied to Addi then left them.

"Come in Dear, there is much to talk about."

Addi sat on the edge of the chair, she couldn't relax until she knew what was going on. Her nails dug into her palms as she tried to look calm.

"Our bloodline is carefully protected. It started many generations ago, Queen Magdaline married for love, they had three children, all born disabled in some form. Her parents blamed her husband for weakening their line; so they searched the area and found a man who was physical perfection and his family had many children, so they knew his seed was strong. He was paid handsomely in return for giving the Queen a perfect heir. They quickly had a child and the man was sent away." Addi was horrified at the idea of being forced to mate with another simply because her children weren't good enough. "That's when our family changed the way things were done. Going forward when an heir was born three children of the same age would be paid to come live in the castle and be the heir's companion. Once the Heir was coming of age, he or she would have to choose which of the three they would marry. The other two would be sent away to live their lives." In a rare show of emotion, her voice hitched. She cleared her throat and continued on, "Beck, Noah, and Dorin were chosen for you. Now that they have returned you will spend time with each of them, then on your birthday, you will announce which one you have chosen."

Addi knew her mouth was wide open, she struggled to comprehend what she was being told. "My father was one of three you chose from?" Addi knew very little of her father, he was rarely spoken of.

A single tear slid down the older woman's cheek. "Yes, I knew Franklin from birth. He was a good man, I was heartbroken when he died."

"Was it hard sending the other two men away?" Addi tried to picture her mom twenty years younger, entertaining three men to choose a husband.

"You are old enough now to know the truth. I loved all three men in my own way, but I didn't want any of them. There was a stable boy, he took my heart from the first day I saw him. Franklin and the other two came back, and I was told I had to make a choice. I was honest with them and begged to be allowed to choose the boy. My father was enraged by this, and the next morning, the boy was gone. It took a while for me to get over him. My mother reminded me of my duty to the Kingdom, so I chose your father and moved on."

Addi's mind was exploding, her mother was always so reserved and a strict follower of the rules. She couldn't picture her rebelling and trying to marry for love. It suddenly became clear why she never seemed to fully accept her. Addi was the child of a man she didn't love. She didn't know who to feel sorrier for, her mother or herself.

Another thought occurred to her, "Is that why I have always been kept from anyone my own age? Every staff member here is much older than me."

"I did it to protect you. I didn't want to put temptation in front of you and risk you falling for someone other than one of the chosen. To be safe, I didn't want to risk one of your boys falling for someone else either, so I made sure there was no one else around."

Years of loneliness finally made sense. At least now Addi understood why she was so isolated. She stared into her mother's eyes and saw emptiness there.

"After my father died, why didn't you go find the stable boy?"

The Queen laughed bitterly, "I've tried, many times. Not because I was going to marry him, I couldn't do that to the crown. I needed to know he was okay, that my father hadn't hurt him. Sadly, he disappeared without a trace."

"What if I don't love one of my chosen?" Addi whispered.

Her face hardened, "You do not have a choice, you have a duty to the crown. Now go spend time with each of them. I expect a decision soon." She stood and left, leaving Addi more confused than she was before.

"But how will I choose?" Addi whispered to the empty room.

Three

Addi's mind was racing, it was bad enough to ask her to choose between her three best friends, but to bring sex and kids into the mix when she was still a virgin was overwhelming. How did her life go from zero to sixty in one day? How did turning eighteen mean she suddenly had to grow up and plan her entire future with a man she hadn't seen in five years?

This is one of those moments in life you wanted to talk to your best friend about what to do or ask your mom for her advice. Unfortunately for Addi, her only friends were at the heart of the issue, and her mother clearly wasn't going to hug her and tell her everything was going to be okay.

She wasn't ready to face the guys, so she went to the one person who always made her feel better.

Marta stood in the kitchen, mixing dough. The older woman took one look at Addi's face, stopped what she was doing, washed her hands quickly then held her arms out.

Addi rushed over and let the older woman console her. "I'm guessing you know the truth now?"

"Everyone knew, didn't they?" Addi mumbled against the woman's shoulder. Tears rolled down her cheeks, she didn't care if Mrs. Parsons walked in at that moment. She had to talk to someone.

Marta pulled away and walked over to the refrigerator. She grabbed a chocolate cake and brought it over to the table. "It's the way it's always been done. If you ask me it's one of many traditions that need to be done away with." She grabbed two forks out of a drawer and sat at the tiny table in the corner. "The rest of the world has moved into the twenty-first century, but your mother likes to keep everything the same as it's always been."

Addi was shocked at Marta's bluntness, no one ever criticized the Queen in front of her. She took a bite of cake and chewed silently so she didn't distract Marta from continuing her diatribe.

"Your mother doesn't allow us to have cell phones inside the castle. I think she's afraid if you experience more of the outside world you'll be harder to control. I've put up with her ways for you, but this is too much. I had really hoped once it came down to actually making you go through with this she would back down rather than make you as bitter as she is."

"It's not just about me, she's asking me to take the right to choose away from one of the guys. They didn't ask for this either, they shouldn't be forced to marry me."

Marta quirked an eyebrow and shook her head. "I have no doubt all three of those boys would do anything for you. If you ask me, it's not the one you choose who will be heartbroken, it's the two you send away."

Nausea overtook Addi, she had just gotten all three back and wasn't ready to let them go already. For a brief second, she hoped that maybe two of them had turned in to total dickheads and it would be easier to choose. She knew she wouldn't be that lucky. It only took five minutes with them earlier to realize they may have changed on the outside but on the inside, they were still her boys. The boys she had cried over when they were taken from her, the ones she had dreamt about and worried about.

The cake sat like a lump in her stomach. Usually, the fudgy goodness cured anything that was bothering her. "Do you really think she'll go through with it? What if I refuse, I'll tell her I'll give up the crown before being forced into this charade of entertaining three guys just to kick two of them out."

Marta's face shifted, Addi could see she had said something to upset her. "You are the only heir to this Kingdom. If the crown were to crumble, what do you think would happen to the thousands of loyal subjects that depend on you?" She pushed her cake plate away. "Your situation is unfortunate. However, it could be so much worse. I promise to help you try to get out of this, but in the end, you have an obligation to your people, and you need to do what is best for the greater good."

Addi's face flushed, she had never been chastised by Marta before, and it hurt. She felt like a selfish fool. "Excuse me." She jumped up to escape before more tears fell.

Marta reached out and grabbed her hand. "I love you as if you were my own. We'll find a way out of this."

Addi nodded and left the kitchen, her emotions were on hyperdrive, and she needed time to think. Needing to escape, she made her way to the West tower. It was the highest point in the castle, and from there she could see for miles around. What she needed right now was perspective.

Four

When it was apparent Addilyn wasn't coming back to talk to them after speaking with the Queen the three guys went their separate ways. Noah went to the one place he always felt closest to Addi, the West Tower.

Over the years, when he was lonely and missing her, he would picture her sitting in the tower looking up at the night sky like they used to do when they were little. They would stare up at the stars, find the biggest, brightest one, and make a wish. They never told each other what they wished for, Addi swore it would mean it wouldn't come true.

He pushed open the door to the tower expecting it to be creaky and dusty from not being used. It swung open easily revealing a small couch with a table and lamp in one corner and a large pile of blankets and pillows under the window. He knew instantly this was still Addi's special hiding place and she had continued coming up here after he left.

The sun shining down on the makeshift bed brought him back to the first time Addi brought him up here.

They were maybe eight years old, Noah had been hiding behind the couch in the library. Addi found him hugging his knees and crying.

"Noah, what's wrong?"

He was embarrassed about getting caught so he wouldn't look at her. "Nothing, I'm fine."

She sat down beside him, her tiny hand grabbed his and held on tight. "If it's okay, I'm going to sit here and be fine too."

Noah glanced up and smiled at her.

She peeked around the couch. "You know this isn't a good hiding place, I have a better one. Come on."

They held hands as she led him up the West Tower. The room was full of boxes and random furniture that hadn't been used in years. Addi pulled him over to the window where she had set up a small blanket and pillow. "No one ever comes up here so you can be fine up here whenever you want."

They laid on the makeshift bed and stared up at the sky. She waited patiently until he gave in and told her why he'd been crying. "I asked the Queen if I could go home and spend the weekend with my mom and dad, I miss them. She told me my duty was to you, and I wasn't allowed to leave, but she'd let me see them soon."

Addi grabbed his hand and squeezed. "I'm sorry you can't be with your family. Do you want me to ask her if you can go?"

He shook his head. "She won't change her mind, it's okay. I'll see them soon."

"As long as you are here you can hide in here whenever you want."

Noah shook the memory away and walked over to a bookshelf in the corner, curious to see what literary works she read. He laughed in appreciation at the titles. His little Addilyn had grown up and was now a bonafide reader of smut. *Scarlet Rose and the Seven Sinners* was worn around the edges, she had obviously read it more than a few times. He grabbed another book and flipped it over. His eyes widened, it was called *Pan's Curse* and apparently, this version had Peter Pan and Captain Hook doing some seriously X-rated things to each other.

The door behind him swung open and slammed against the wall. Addi rushed in and threw herself down on the blankets. Her sobs broke his heart, she obviously didn't take the news well. He considered walking out and leaving her in peace, but he couldn't leave her in pain.

He walked over quietly and knelt down. "Addilyn..."

She yelped and rolled over, it took a second for her to recognize him. "Noah, what are you doing in here?" She wiped the tears from her eyes and straightened her dress.

He glanced out the window for a second before looking back at her. "I was feeling a little lost and thought I could hide out here for a bit. I see you still come up here." He held the pirate book up and waved it at her. Her face turned five shades of purple, her eyes were wide. "It's okay, I'm just teasing you."

She reached up to try to pull the book from his hand, he held on tight. "That is Shawna's, I was letting her keep it here so she could read when she had free time."

Noah didn't believe her, there were way too many similar titles on the bookcase. "And who is Shawna?"

"Oh right, she came after you left. She's my maid turned companion. She's our age, you'll like her a lot."

He let go of the book and let her shove it under one of the pillows. "If this is the kind of stuff she likes to read than I'm sure she'll get along with us really well." He stood up, "I didn't mean to intrude, I'll leave you to your privacy."

He turned and was pulled back by her tiny hand, grabbing his. "Please stay, sit with me?"

For a brief second, he thought about Beck and Dorin, would they mind if he talked to her first? Her large green eyes were still bright with unshed tears, he couldn't walk away if he wanted to.

He knelt down and turned to lay next to her. Like when they were little, she immediately curled up next to him and put her head on his shoulder.

She glanced up at him. "Is this okay?"

For a few seconds, he didn't answer, he took a deep breath, her scent bringing back memories and stirring new emotions. "Of course, it is." He wrapped one arm around her, his thumb making lazy circles on her arm.

She picked up the necklace he was wearing, her fingers traced the crest. "Where did you get this?"

There was so much she didn't know but had a right to be told. "All three of us have one. It signifies our allegiance to you. Basically, it lets people know we are spoken for and were protected by the crown. It actually came in handy a few times when fights were brewing while we were at school." He left out the part where it was also a shining neon light to women warning *hands-off*. Not that any of them had any desire to sleep around while they were gone, most women ran from them, afraid to piss off the crown. Not that they were inexperienced virgins, they were given private lessons in the art of pleasure.

Noah hadn't minded when the lessons were theoretical, but once it came to hands-on, all three of them had been hesitant. It's not that they weren't horny. They were loyal to Addilyn and didn't feel right doing it.

They were told it was their responsibility to keep their future Queen satisfied in every way. Once they came to terms with the fact that they were expected to be fluent in the art of seduction, they gave in and learned what they needed to.

"I'm sorry my mother has done this to you. She had no right to take you from your families and force you to be here."

"Addi, it's okay really..."

She shook her head against his chest. "No, it's not. What if you dreamt of traveling the world or being a doctor? Instead, you were taken from your families, shipped off to school, and now are back here being forced to compete to marry someone you don't even know."

Noah was taken aback by her vehemence, she had no idea how much he worshipped her. If she chose him, he would spend every breath in service to her.

He grabbed her chin and forced her to look up at him. "Over the last five years, we counted the days until we could return to you. There is nowhere on Earth we would rather be than here with you. I know Dorin and Beck feel the same way, we've talked about you more times than I care to admit."

His body felt like it was on fire, she was inches from his face. He wanted to pull her on top of him and kiss her sadness away.

She smiled sweetly then laid her head back down, his heart felt like it was beating out of his chest. Waiting for her to pick was going to be the most painfully frustrating experience of his life.

Five

Addi almost died when Noah found her books, she didn't mind him being in her private sanctuary, it was initially their hiding place, to begin with. But what kind of a first impression was it for him to find those and that is the first thing he learns about her after all this time?

Poor Shawna, she felt terrible throwing her under the bus when the books weren't even hers, Addi panicked, and now Noah probably thought the girl was some kind of sex fiend.

She had laid with Noah for a while, listening to him talk about what they had done while they were away at school. She didn't admit it out loud, but she was jealous they got to have those experiences without her.

It wasn't until the sun started going down did they part ways so she could get ready for dinner. He had walked her to her bedroom door then continued on to the room directly to her left. Goosebumps danced across her skin thinking about him being on the other side of the wall and her mother being on a completely different floor of the castle.

She may not have any actual experiences with guys, but she had read enough to be able to imagine the possibilities of their current setup. Then again, that would be playing right into her mother's hands, and she didn't want to give in that easily.

The door to her room opened, Shawna stood on the other side with a huge smile on her face. She pulled Addi in and pushed her onto the bed. "Oh my god, start talking now."

Addi played innocent. "What am I supposed to be talking about?"

The other girl rolled her eyes, "I saw them arrive, I found out why they are here, start talking."

Addi blushed, apparently, her sex life was the topic of the day. "They were my best friends growing up, they are back now, and we're getting to know each other again."

"You forget I grew up in town, I know the men around here. You have been given gods to choose from." Shawna fanned herself. "It really isn't fair that you get to be Princess *and* get to fuck the three hottest guys our country has ever produced."

Addi laughed at her friend's curse word. If Mrs. Parson's heard her, she would throw the girl out of the castle immediately. God forbid Addi have any sense of a normal teenage life. Thank god, her friend was brave and treated her like a normal girl when they were alone.

"Perhaps you should join us for dinner, I have a feeling my mother isn't going to be in attendance. She is dead set that I choose one of them immediately."

Shawna ate with Addi whenever the Queen was away or unavailable, her mother would love to know she brought her along to meet the guys. It would probably piss her off to know Addi was bringing another girl along who might distract one of the guys. Addi wasn't worried though, she wanted what was best for all of them, and if fate decided Shawna was supposed to be with one of them, she wouldn't stop it.

"You want me to eat with them?" Shawna's face lost all color.

"Grab one of my dresses and get changed, I am starving, and between you and me, I really do want to spend time with them so let's go."

***

Shawna had a death grip on Addi's hand, she acted as if she had never been alone with a hot guy before, and Addi knew precisely how she felt.

As they walked into the dining room side by side, all three men were already inside waiting for them. They quickly stood and bowed towards them. That was new, and Addi didn't like it, they had never been formal with her before even though Mrs. Parsons had threatened to punish them on more than one occasion.

She waved at them to sit down then made her way to her seat. Shawna sat on her right, and the guys sat across from them. "Gentleman, you look handsome tonight. I would like you all to meet my best friend, Shawna Capland." She reached over and brushed the hair off the other girl's face and tucked it behind her ear. Addi hated that she hid her face when she was around anyone new. She was beautiful, and anyone that felt differently had no need to be a part of their lives. "Shawna, I would like you to meet Dorin, Beck, and Noah."

Noah stood and bowed directly at Shawna, "It's lovely to meet you. I've heard a lot about you."

Addi scowled at him, she would kick him under the table if he mentioned the books.

Beck stood next and followed suit. "Thank you for taking care of our girl while we were away."

A shiver of excitement rolled down Addi's spine when he called her *their girl*.

Dorin stood last, he was the tallest and the unofficial leader of their motley crew. "We were worried about Ducky being alone while we were gone. We're in your debt for being there for her when we couldn't be."

The other two men nodded agreement. Addi wanted to yell at him about the nickname, but his sweet words and declaration to Shawna had her feeling like a pile of mush.

Shawna's face turned bright pink, she hadn't had so much attention at one time in her life, and the fact that all three men ignored her physical imperfections made Addi love them even more. "Beck, I actually know your family. My family lives near yours, I grew up playing with your brothers and sisters."

Addi gasped, she knew Dorin had a little sister, but she didn't realize the other two might have siblings as well. "I thought you were an only child?"

Beck shrugged, "I don't know them well, they are a few years younger than us. I was already living here when they were born."

Addi felt her anger at her mother growing into rage. She turned to Noah and gave him a questioning look.

He fiddled with his fork as he looked down and answered. "I have two little sisters." He pointed over at Dorin. "He has a few brothers too."

Addi was horrified to know they didn't know their own brothers and sisters simply because of her mother's archaic need to control the gene pool.

Shawna leaned forward to get everyone's attention. "I am so sorry I said something, I shouldn't have come. I'll leave now."

Addi reached over and grabbed her hand. "Please don't leave, I'm not mad at anyone in this room." She took a deep breath before continuing. "I can't tell you how many times I've wished for siblings, especially after the three of you left. To know you've missed out on growing up with yours makes me angry for you."

Dorin shook his head at her. "We've gotten to see them a couple of times a year, and honestly we grew up with you not them, it's hard to miss people that you don't really know."

"I don't accept knowing you have siblings I haven't met. Why don't we host a lunch here on Saturday and you can invite all of them, Shawna you can bring your brother and sister as well."

Noah laughed, "I'm not sure I'll get one of my sisters to come, she refuses to wear dresses, and you know your mother won't allow her to wear pants to the castle."

"She can't say anything if it's a pool party. They can be driven around to the pool house, no one will need to be paraded through the castle. Sound good?"

She looked at each person and waited for them to agree, not that she expected anyone to refuse her. There were a few perks to being the Princess.

Once the plans were decided, she waved at the server in the corner to start the meal. The tension in the room instantly lessened.

Over the next hour, the guys took turns telling stories about each other and the stupid things they did at school. Addi had forgotten what it was like to hang out with them, her heart squeezed at the idea that soon she would be losing two of them.

Six

Dorin couldn't sleep, he was back under the same roof as Addilyn, and he was expected to fight his two best friends to win her. If it were anyone else, he would slay them in an instant. Addi had been his for as long as he could remember. Even before they knew what their real purpose for being there was, he knew he was going to be with her forever.

Asking him to go against Beck and Noah was cruel, for the last five years, he'd thought of little else except figuring out how to be with Addi and not hurt the guys in the process. The problem was, he knew they felt the same way, and that was the crux of the problem. He had been considering walking away and letting one of them have her but now that he had seen her again and the beauty she had grown into there was no way he was giving up.

When it came time for her to decide, he didn't know how the two who weren't chosen would react. It would likely take the Queen's guard forcibly removing them to get rid of them. For the last seventeen years he was raised to be loyal to her then one day he may simply be dismissed and sent on his way. He couldn't even imagine what he would do with himself if that happened.

Frustrated with the whole situation, he got up and made his way out of the castle. He always had preferred animals over people, and it was no different now. He entered the stable, the dogs who lived there with the stable master barked once then stopped when they saw him.

"Max, Mirabella, it's me. You're safe." The dogs ran over, tails wagging. He was excited to see six puppies trailing behind them. "Well now, you've been busy while I was gone, haven't you?"

He sat down by a pole and leaned against it. All his heartache disappeared as he was mauled with kisses.

The smell of hay brought back a memory of when he was ten.

Dorin was sitting on the fence watching Niles exercise the horses. Out of the corner of his eye, he saw Addi walking out of the trees holding something, she was sobbing. He ran to her. "Addi, what happened?

She held her hands out and opened them. "Is it dead?"

A baby bird was lying still, it was obviously gone. "What happened?"

She sniffled loudly. "I was climbing a tree to look in the nest, and I knocked it out. It was an accident, I swear." Her eyes were huge, he could see she was genuinely upset.

He scooped the bird out of her hands. "I know you didn't mean it. Let's get a box, and we can bury it."

She cried the entire way to the barn quietly. She grabbed hay and put it in the box he had found so it would have a soft place to lay. They walked back out to the woods and buried it in the middle of a flower patch.

Their hands were covered in dirt, but she grabbed his anyways and squeezed. "Thank you for helping me."

They snuck into the kitchen, and Marta helped them clean up before anyone saw them.

"Imagine my surprise when I saw you walking in here."

He glanced up to see Addi leaning against the door frame smiling at him. "I couldn't sleep." He shrugged.

"I see you've met the B's." She walked over and sat next to him, half the puppies immediately jumped on her lap to lick her.

"Why are they the B's?"

"We had a litter two years ago, and they all had A names. This time they were all given names that started with B's." She pointed to the two who were tugging on his shoelaces. "That is Boe and Buster, they are the troublemakers of the group." She pointed to the two wrestling on his lap. "That is Beatrice and Brock, they beg for attention all the time and can sniff out food a mile away."

Dorin grabbed the pup who was running circles around them and tripping over its feet constantly. "What about this one?" He held it up to his face and kissed its snout.

"That poor guy is Bumper, aptly named because he has no coordination." She snuggled the last puppy against her neck. "And this sweetie is Bitsy, she was the runt of the litter and wasn't expected to make it. She's tougher than they thought and showed them."

He watched her snuggle her nose against the pup and kiss it, he was never more jealous of an animal as he was in that moment. Forget the fact that it was also snugly pressed against her breasts. He cleared his throat and looked away.

"Are you planning to keep any of them?"

Addi gave him a sad smile. "I tried to keep one of the A's, but mother said it wasn't allowed in the castle. Shawna took him home, sometimes she brings him here so I can see him."

People were always jealous of the Princess. They had no idea how lonely an existence she truly had. "How are you doing with all of this?"

Her eyes met his, he wasn't sure if he overstepped.

"It's a dream come true to have you all home, but all the rest of it feels like a nightmare I can't wake up from. Two days ago, my biggest concern was deciding what special meal Marta was going to make for me on my birthday. Now I'm expected to make a rash decision about something that is going to affect me for the rest of my life."

He reached over and brushed the tear from her cheek. "We don't want to hurt you. Whatever you decide we'll go along with it. I don't care what the Queen says, we listen to you. If you want us to leave, we'll do that too."

She grabbed his hand, panic in her eyes. "No, don't leave me again. I can't lose you again." She turned to face him, her teeth nibbled her bottom lip for a few seconds. "Will you give me my first kiss?"

Dorin instantly hardened, he assumed she was an innocent but never dreamed she wouldn't have had at least kissed someone before. He didn't expect the excitement it gave him knowing he would be her first, even if it was only a kiss.

He straightened his legs out, "Come here." He pulled her on top of him, so she was straddling his lap. He stroked his fingers up her arm then brushed her hair back from her forehead. Her chest was rapidly rising and falling, he liked that she stared straight into his eyes even though she was near panting with nerves.

He curled his hand around her neck and pulled her face close to his. "Close your eyes." With complete trust, her lids fluttered closed. He started at her forehead and gently kissed her warm, soft skin. Her lips parted as he got closer to her mouth, he smiled as he moved lower and kissed the smooth, pale skin of her neck. He traced small circles with his tongue before lightly sucking. She moaned and ran her fingers through his hair, holding him close. She sucked her bottom lip between her teeth, he could feel the heat growing between her legs. If she moved an inch, she was going to feel exactly how much he wanted to kiss her.

"Please." She whispered.

He made his way up to her mouth, he caught her bottom lip between his and sucked lightly before letting go and kissing her. She leaned into him, trying to rush the moment. He pulled back slightly, kissed her softly a few more times before turning her head and sliding his tongue against hers.

After that, he was lost, he stopped thinking and enjoyed her quiet moans, and the feel of her chest pressed against him.

A long, skinny, wet tongue came up and licked their faces. They both jerked away, Max stared at them, excited to be a part of the action.

Damn dog.

Addi's eyes were still clouded with lust, her hand was resting on her lips. This was a colossal mistake, one taste of her, and it sealed his fate. He would do whatever it took to stay with her.

Seven

Addi growled at Shawna as she came in her room to help her get ready for breakfast. After her kiss with Dorin in the stable the night before, he walked her back to her room, kissed her gently then went to his room directly across the hall from her.

Addi was so wound up she had struggled to sleep. Around four a.m. she had relented and pulled out the Christmas present from Shawna that had been hidden in her closet. She had thought Addi needed help relaxing and bought her a vibrator. Addi was so mortified she had hidden it away and not touched it again until now.

It had taken a couple of minutes trying different things before she figured out how it felt best then she rode the wave twice before finally falling asleep.

Now she was kicking herself that she had waited so long to pleasure herself. She had been missing out and kind of wanted to slap Shawna for not pushing her harder to try it. It would have been an awkward conversation, but now that Addi understood the outcome it was one she would have been grateful for.

Shawna pulled the window curtains back to let a little light in. "Looks like you had a rough night. Dinner didn't sit well with you?"

Addi threw her arm over her eyes to block out the light. "I may have had a run-in with one of the guys last night."

She was pitched to the side as Shawna jumped on the bed squealing. "Which one? Tell me every detail."

Addi smiled. "It was Dorin, and he kissed me."

Shawna shoved her. "Shut up. Damn girl, you move quick."

"I happened to walk by the window and saw him walking towards the stable, so I followed him out there. We were talking and playing with the dogs then I asked him to kiss me and boy did he."

Her skin warmed, thinking about his lips on her.

Shawna's jaw dropped. "You asked him? I have a whole new level of respect for you, I did not expect that."

"I didn't plan it when I went down there, I just wanted to talk to him. He was sitting on the ground playing with the puppies, and he said he would defy my mother and do whatever I asked of him and it was too much for me." She shivered from the memory of his lips on her. "I always knew he would be my first kiss."

Shawna launched herself forward and hugged Addi. "I know this isn't the best situation, but I am happy for you." She sat back. "Who's next, and what are you going to do with them?"

"You make it sound so perfunctory, maybe I should line them up and take turns kissing them."

"Screw that, you are literally surrounded by them. I say you move from room to room until you get what you want out of them then make your decision."

Addi blushed. She couldn't imagine bouncing from room to room, sleeping with them then moving on to the next one.

A knock on the door had Shawna jumping up to answer it. She spoke to someone quietly then went to Addi's closet to pick a dress out. "The Queen would like a word with you before breakfast."

Addi rolled her eyes, she had no doubt what the subject of their conversation would be. "Let's get this over with, I'm starving and want to get back to the guys."

***

Addi knocked on the door to her mother's suite. Liza bowed as she opened the door then left them alone.

Addi found her mother sitting under an umbrella on her balcony. "Good morning, Mother."

"Did you enjoy your reunion yesterday?"

Addi sat down in the chair next to her and looked out over the garden. "I am grateful they are back, I truly did miss them."

"From what I hear, you spent quite a bit of time with Noah but had more fun with Dorin. Should I assume you are leaning his way? I can go ahead and send Beck away now if narrowing it down will make it easier for you."

Rage rushed through Addi. "You are spying on me? How can you be so callous about a man's life? They are not here for you to play God with."

Ellena, her mother was gone, the icy stare of Ellena the Queen turned sharply and glared at her. "You will not speak to me in that tone, remember your place." Her eyes flicked back over to the garden before continuing. "Your reason for being is to be Queen and to rule fairly for your people. You will produce heirs that will continue our traditions, and they need to be of premium stock. Take your emotions out of it and grow up. It's time for you to realize your purpose in life and accept it."

Addi felt as if she had been slapped, her mother had never been affectionate with her, but right now, she was downright evil. She stood to leave, she didn't want to spend another minute in her mother's presence.

She was stopped cold by the warning her mother tossed out. "I heard about you parading

Shawna in front of the guys. Once you've chosen you can toss your leftovers to her. Until then keep her away, or I will send her away permanently."

Addi's spine was straight as a rod as she walked out, she wasn't going to let her mother see the tears streaming down her face.

Eight

Beck dove into the lake, the cold water tingling against his hot skin. He could have gone swimming in the pool house, but he wanted to be alone, and that was the one thing you couldn't get in the palace. There were always eyes watching.

His lungs were burning by the time he popped his head above the water. He had always been good at swimming, his lung capacity was impressive, no one at school could ever come close.

Being back in the lake brought back him back to the last time he swam in there.

It was a couple of weeks before they were sent away. He had always preferred swimming here instead of the pool house. Addi had come with him that day, and after a while of floating and hanging out, she challenged him to a race back to shore.

He knew he could easily win, but she was headstrong and always desperate to show she could do anything they could do. He agreed to the race and even let her take a head start. He overtook her and was close to winning when he faked a leg cramp and let her win.

She jumped out of the water, made sure he was okay then danced around celebrating her win.

The entire way back to the castle she gloated about beating him, he loved seeing her beam with pride. His little Princess was always full of fire.

He turned to swim back to shore and spotted Addi as she burst through the tree line. She collapsed into a ball, sobbing. He took off and rushed out of the water.

She looked up shocked to see him running out of the water. "Where did you come from?"

"I'm really a merman, you disrupted me in my home."

She laughed, tears still streaming down her cheeks. He kneeled in front of her, careful not to drip on her.

"What happened?"

She shook her head, angrily wiping her face. "The evil Queen is fucking with my mind, and I let her get the better of me."

Beck was taken back by her language, he'd never heard Addi say any swear word let alone when talking about her mother. "I guess she didn't get better after we left?"

Addi scoffed. "I never knew why she treated me so coldly, now I do. My father was one of her three chosen ones. Plot twist, she loved someone else, and he was taken from her. She basically said she couldn't love me because I wasn't the daughter of the man she loved."

Beck wanted to hug her, she looked like a lost child. He may not get to spend much time with his parents, but at least he knew they loved him. "You deserve better than her. No matter which of us you choose I hope you know we will love you and our children with every ounce of our beings."

Addi's eyes met his, for a second, he didn't know what she was thinking or how she was feeling about him saying they loved her.

She reached up and brushed a curl of hair from his forehead. "I'm the one who doesn't deserve all of you." She got up on her knees and leaned forward. Her lips tentatively met his, he could tell she wasn't very confident. He let her explore for a few more seconds, her tongue tentatively brushing against his. He turned his head and deepened the kiss. She tasted as good as she smelled. His shorts instantly tightened, there was not going to be any way to hide it, and his towel was halfway around the lake.

He pulled back and leaned his forehead against hers, they gasped for breath.

"Take me swimming with you."

He glanced down at her dress. "Do you wear bathing suits under your dresses?"

She reached behind her and unzipped the gown. His mouth went dry.

She stood and let it pool around her feet. All the lust in the world didn't drive out her training though. She grabbed the garment and laid it nicely on a dry patch of grass. She stood shyly in her light pink bra and underwear, her arms clutched across her stomach.

He stood and held his hand out to her, she glanced down at the tent he was pitching and smiled at him. They walked into the cold water, she shivered when the water went between her legs. After the kiss they shared he wouldn't be surprised if she was significantly warmer there.

They stopped when she could no longer fully touch the bottom, she surprised him by wrapping her arms and legs around him and holding on. He loved the boldness she was starting to show.

He grabbed her hips and pulled her tight against his erection. His eyes closed briefly, need roared through his veins, he wanted her, and it was going to be painful to go slow.

She kissed his neck, her tongue trailed up to his ear and took the lobe between her lips. He moaned, she was going to be the death of him. She whispered in his ear. "Touch me, please."

His eyes opened, he studied her for a second before giving in to what they both wanted. He grabbed her hair and wrapped it around his hand.

He tugged her head back and kissed a trail from her mouth down to her breasts. Her nipples were straining against the wet silk of her bra. He took one in his mouth and sucked gently. She gasped, her fingers wrapped through his hair.

He moved to the other nipple, his tongue flicked it a few times before he reached up and pulled her breast free of the cup. The tiny bud bobbed in and out of the water, he took it in his mouth and sucked, his other hand let go of her hair, he grabbed her other nipple and pinched. The harder he sucked, the more she rocked against his cock. He needed to slip inside her, but knowing she was innocent helped him control the need burning inside him.

He couldn't hold back much longer, he let go of her nipple with his hand and moved it down between them. His thumb found her clit, he moaned at the heat radiating from her.

He sucked her breast and rubbed circles on her clit until she was screaming out his name.

Hearing her call for him was satisfaction enough until he could get back to his room and take care of himself. Even if the walk was going to be painful.

She rested her head in the crook of his neck. For a few minutes, he held her and let her catch her breath. He stroked the soft skin of her back, he loved feeling her wrapped around him. How was he going to let her go if she didn't choose him?

Nine

Addi was restless. Now that she knew the Queen was spying on her and watching her progress with the guys she wanted nothing more than to avoid the castle at all costs. She wanted to find one of the guys and see what they were doing, but every time she was alone with one of them, she ended up a wet, hot mess, and she felt guilty. It's not cheating when she really wasn't with any of them. That still didn't make her feel better about fooling around with all of them.

Do they talk about her when she wasn't around? Did they admit what she had done with each of them? The idea had her warring between mortification and excitement.

The door to the study swung open, Noah popped his head inside. He smiled when he found her curled in a chair by the window. "Somehow I knew if you weren't up in your private library, you would be here."

He walked in and scanned the books lining the shelves. "I was thinking about going for a ride.

That is assuming Niles lets me step inside the barn."

Addi laughed, memories of an eight-year-old Noah yelling as he clung on to the horse he was riding and trying not to fall. His saddle had been loose, and it had slipped to the side. Niles had rushed out and stopped the animal. He yelled at Noah for ten minutes about responsibility and forbid him from ever coming near the horses again.

"If you hadn't taken his favorite mare out, he might've been more understanding."

He gave her an exasperated look. "He told me I wasn't allowed to leave the barn until I could saddle a horse on my own. She was the shortest animal in the barn, I was trying to be practical. If I hadn't been starving, I might have been a little more patient." He rubbed the back of his neck as he laughed about the memory. "In my defense, I did technically saddle the horse and ride it for a few yards so I shouldn't have been punished."

Addi stood and walked towards him. "If you are going to ask Niles if you can ride then I'm coming along, I wouldn't miss this."

She rolled her eyes as he pretended to be offended. "I'll have you know I was top in our class at school in riding. I just needed a few extra inches of height and more muscle." He crossed his arms and looked down at her. "You can only come to watch me grovel if you agree to come riding with me?"

"Give me two minutes to change." She ran from the room and took the stairs quickly. As soon as her bedroom door closed, she was pulling her dress off and switching to riding pants and a shirt. She laced up her boots and made her way back to Noah.

He sat in the chair she had vacated, thumbing through a book. He glanced up, his jaw dropped. "Are you trying to kill Mrs. Parsons?"

Addi was confused for a second before realization dawned on her. "Some things have changed since you left. After a near-death experience involving riding in my dress, Mother agreed to let me wear pants. She wasn't happy, but I played up the injuries enough that she didn't want to risk her heir over something so inconsequential." She shrugged, "When we have guests I still have to wear a dress. Since those rides are usually slow and boring I don't argue."

She knew she was rambling, but he hadn't stopped running his gaze up and down her body and she had goosebumps running up and down her back at the look on his face. It only took a couple of days with the guys to recognize lust.

She had been wondering if he had wanted her like the other two did, the answer was clearly written in his expression.

He stood and walked over to her. He stroked one hand up her arm to her face. His thumb stroked her cheek as he looked into her eyes. "I suddenly have no desire to go anywhere."

Addi's mouth went dry, even though she had orgasmed that morning with Beck in the lake, she could feel the heat pooling in her lower belly. She didn't want to leave either, but prying eyes were everywhere. "How about we go for a short ride, and we can take a break somewhere in the woods...where we'll be alone."

Noah's eyes closed, he leaned his head back for a second. He let out a deep breath and cleared his throat. "I can't promise we'll make it very far before I make you stop, but I'll try."

Addi laughed as she grabbed his hand and pulled him along. They walked the short distance to the barn, she was relieved they didn't see the other two guys, she would have been torn over inviting them when she wanted to be alone with Noah.

He opened the door and let her walk in first. Niles stood in the center of the room, brushing down one of the Queen's mares. "Princess, are you back to play with the dogs?"

Addi's face turned bright red, she glanced at Noah out of the corner of her eye. Before she could respond, Niles caught sight of Noah.

The older man crossed his arms and scowled. "So, you think you're ready to step back in here?"

"I swear on my life I have learned from my mistakes and would never harm any animal."

The stable master didn't move or make a sound.

"You can watch me saddle whatever horse you want and if you aren't satisfied I'll walk away."

Niles scratched his chin as he sized up the younger man. "Fine. Let's see how you do with Titan."

Addi gasped. "Niles, no..."

Noah laid a hand on her shoulder. "It's okay, have faith in me."

She closed her mouth, if he wanted to kill himself trying to prove something then let him.

The trio made their way to the back of the barn and out to the fenced enclosure behind it. The jet-black stallion stood in the center chewing on hay.

The animal caught sight of them and instantly reared up. The horse was wild, and even though Niles had been working with him for almost a month, he hadn't gotten anywhere.

Noah slowly walked toward the horse, it stomped its feet warning him away. He talked quietly to it, his hand held out so the horse could sniff him when it was ready. His movements were painfully slow, eventually, he made it two feet away. Titan had stopped pouncing on the ground. Addi could see it was still sizing him up. He leaned his hand up towards its face, the animal reared up and whinnied again. Addi would have run. Noah continued whispering, waiting for Titan to calm down.

When it dropped to the ground again, it reached out and sniffed his hand then pulled back. Noah reached into his pockets and pulled something out. Addi couldn't see what was happening, but Titan was repeatedly going up to his hand and pulling back.

Noah walked over to the fence and grabbed a saddle that was hanging over the side. He went back to cooing to the horse as he walked towards it again. Titan tossed his head a couple of times but stayed still otherwise.

Noah brushed his hand down the horse's neck multiple times before setting the saddle on his back.

"Always trust the instincts of an animal. If it trusts a person than you know they are decent.

For that horse to trust that boy must mean he is pretty special. He'd make you a fine King one day."

Addi turned surprised eyes to the older man. She still couldn't get past everyone knowing about her current predicament. She wouldn't be surprised if there were a betting pool going on which one she would pick.

Noah walked back over and joined them, a triumphant smile on his face. "I hope you will find everything to your satisfaction." He stood back to let the other man inspect Titan.

"No need son, I haven't managed to get the saddle on him yet, so you've gotten farther than me already. You can ride any horse inside, except the Queen's."

Noah nodded and led Addi back inside. He walked along the stalls glancing inside each one. "Do you have a favorite?"

Addi walked over and stood in front of a stall with the name *Valliant* on a sign above it. The horse was pure white except for the lowest section of his legs, which were brown. It came to the door and rubbed its nose against Addi's shoulder. He'd always been affectionate with her.

Noah let the horse sniff his hand before he reached up and scratched its neck. "Who should I ride?"

Addi glanced around, then pointed to a stall a few doors down. "Deloris loves men, she'd probably enjoy getting attention from you."

Noah walked over and laughed. "Are you sure she can keep up with Valliant?"

Addi stood next to him and glanced in at the black and white spotted mare. She was the tiniest horse they owned, but that didn't mean anything. She was full of fire, and Addi often rode her when she was feeling the need to sprint.

She glanced over at a groomsman who had been cleaning out a stall nearby. "Can you ready Valliant for me?"

Noah grabbed a lead rope and led Deloris to the center and put her tack on. Addi couldn't help smiling as the mare nuzzled Noah's neck. She was throwing herself at him, he continually stopped to give her attention then went back to get her ready.

Niles was right, the way a man was with animals said a lot about his character.

***

"Holy shit, Deloris is my new love." Noah stood in the center of the clearing scratching between the mare's eyes.

When they first started riding, they had walked for a bit. Once Addi nudged Valliant into a run, Deloris took off, she wasn't about to let the other horse win. Addi had almost fallen because she was laughing so hard at the look of shock on Noah's face. It hadn't taken him long to get a feel for her and urge her on. They were a perfectly cohesive unit, he had leaned down close to her neck and let her run free.

By the time they had reached the clearing in the woods, they were all slightly out of breath. Noah had jumped off, his cheeks flush with excitement.

He walked over and helped Addi slide down off Valliant before he tied both horses to a tree and took off their saddles. They were lathered in sweat, Addi appreciated that he took the time to take care of the horses before grabbing a blanket out of a saddlebag and walking over to her.

They laid side by side on the blanket and stared up at the bits of blue sky that were peaking between the tree branches.

He rolled onto his side, facing her and rested his head in his hand. "You seem better than you were the other day. Have you come to terms with all this yet?"

She didn't look over at him as she answered. "I'm still pissed at my mother. If I'm being honest though, I wouldn't want to marry anyone but one of you so I should be thankful you are all so willing to be with me." She glanced over, tears burned her eyes. "I don't know how I'm going to choose."

He reached up and brushed her hair off her forehead. "When it's time, your heart will know which one of us is the right one. Don't stress over it, right now all you need to do is spend time with us, let us jump through your mother's hoops then at the ball you can let yourself think about the choice. I think you'll find it remarkably easy to decide."

Addi wished it were that simple. When she spent time with one of them, it felt right. One didn't feel more right than the others. If she was really going to compare them, then she had to do the same things with all of them.

She leaned up and kissed him. His eyes widened in surprise for a second before he partially rolled on top of her and kissed her back. Just like when she kissed Dorin and Beck, she instantly reacted, her skin tingled, her nipples hardened, and she wanted more. But she wasn't sure what to ask for.

She put her hand on his chest and pushed slightly, he pulled back and looked at her through haze filled eyes. "So, those books you saw...I want to experience all of it." She could see some emotion swirling in his eyes. "Will you...um...go down there." She pointed down between them. She was never so embarrassed in her life, but she needed to experience everything before making a choice.

He smiled, "With pleasure."

He leaned down and kissed her as his hand made its way down to her shirt. He undid each button; her breasts were aching with need. He hooked a finger and thumb around her bra between her breasts and tugged upward, so they slid out from the bottom.

She reached down to take her boots off. He pushed her back. "Let me take care of you." He undid the zippers on the side of each shoe and pulled them off.

She was shaking with nerves as he climbed on top of her. She instinctively opened her legs and let him rest between them. He kissed down her neck, grabbing a breast in each hand he gently squeezed them together and buried his face between them. He moved from one to the other kissing everywhere except her nipples. It was almost painful waiting for him to take one in his mouth.

He let go of one and moved down to her pants, he quickly undid the button and zipper. As his hand dipped insider her panties and found her throbbing clit, he latched on to her nipple. She bucked against him, he held on until she was begging for more. She didn't know what the more was but her body told her she needed it.

She whimpered as he pushed up onto his knees, she instantly missed his weight on top of her. He grabbed her ankles and put them on his shoulders. His mouth found the ticklish spot on her instep, she couldn't help laughing. He hooked each pointer finger in the waistband above her hips and pulled her pants and underwear down to her ankles and pulled one foot out.

He dropped her feet back on the ground and pushed her knees apart, so she was spread wide. It dawned on her he had a full view of her, and she wasn't sure how to feel about it. He grabbed her thighs just below her pussy and squeezed. "You are perfect in every way."

His fingers found her opening, and he slowly inserted one finger. Her hands bunched into the blanket, the feelings were more intense than she expected. He inserted a second finger and started pumping them in and out. Her hips naturally thrust against his hand. Their rhythm sped up until she was gasping for breath.

At some point, while her eyes were closed, he had laid down between her legs. He kissed the inside of one thigh then the other. She tensed, nervous about what was going to happen next. He gently kissed her mound; his hot breath sent a shiver down her back. She dug her heels into the ground and lifted her hips. He chuckled against her, the vibration making her moan.

His tongue drew a small circle at her entrance then licked up to her clit. He rolled the nub around a few times, she whispered his name as he latched on and sucked. Her back came off the ground, her thighs closed against his head, it was shocking.

He let up and went back to long, slow licks. As he made his way back to her clit, he latched on at the same time as he inserted two fingers. She lost the ability to focus on what he was doing. She rode the wave as it built and screamed as she came against him. He locked his arms around her thighs and held on, drinking every drop of her orgasm.

As she came down and started to relax, he laid his head against her thigh and kissed her gently. Her fingers found his head, and she pulled gently. She wanted his weight back on top of her.

He climbed back up and settled on top of her. She could feel his erection against her, while she was scared of actually having sex for the first time she was tempted to ask him to slide inside her.

He kissed her temple. "Are you okay?"

She peeked one eye open then the other. "Are you serious? I'm on cloud nine right now. That was the most amazing thing I have ever felt." Obviously, she had few experiences to compare, but she wasn't lying.

He smiled, she could see the pride on his face. Is it wrong she hoped the other two wouldn't be as good as he was at that? It would certainly sway things his way if she got to have that for the rest of their lives.

Ten

Saturday morning Addi was jumping out of bed excited to get the day started. The guy's siblings were coming for the pool party, and she couldn't wait to meet all of them. Not to mention, she had almost no experience hanging out with people her age, so she was eager to be normal for a day.

Her bedroom door opened, Shawna came in quietly expecting Addi to still be asleep. She walked over to the closet to start pulling out clothes.

"I've already got my clothes out." Addi laughed, watching the other girl jump and yelp.

Shawna had her hand over her chest. "You scared the crap out of me. I didn't see you."

Addi shrugged. "I woke up early so I figured I would get ready. I'm heading down to breakfast then over to the pool house." She stood up and smoothed out the simple dress she had tossed on. "You brought your bathing suit, right?"

"My sister is bringing my stuff. I'll get changed over there."

Addi walked to the bed and picked up the small tote bag that had her bathing suit in it. "I'll see you over there."

Addi made her way to the dining room. Her mood changed when she saw her mother sitting at the table with the guys. She straightened her back and walked in quietly. All three men immediately stopped talking and stood, waiting for her to sit.

The Queen looked at her outfit and quirked a questioning eyebrow at her. She chose to ignore her and not explain it was twenty-nineteen, she shouldn't have to wear formal gowns every day.

Addi looked at each man and smiled at them. "Good morning, everyone." She was surprised how awkward she felt having all three of them in the same room considering what she'd done with each of them.

Beck winked at her. Noah bowed his head to her, and Dorin reached under the table and squeezed her hand which had been gripping her dress.

Her mother cleared her throat to get everyone's attention. "It's my understanding you are having guests over today. I'll let you have your fun today. Tomorrow we start the first challenge." The group exchanged glances with each other. Addi didn't really believe they were going to be put through any trials.

Dorin set his fork down. "Do we get to know what it is we'll be doing?"

The Queen smiled sweetly at him. "Of course, how you prepare speaks volumes for your character." Addi rolled her eyes. "Tomorrow will be an obstacle course through the woods on horseback." Three sets of eyes landed on Noah. Apparently, the other two guys knew that was going to be Noah's strong suit.

"The next contest will be held at the cliffs. You'll start at the bottom, first to climb to the top will win." Addi wasn't sure which guy would be better suited for that competition. Dorin and Noah did because they glanced at Beck. When they were swimming the other day Addi had taken notice of his upper body strength, she could see how that could help him.

"If Addi still needs help with her decision we'll have a third contest. It will be hand to hand combat." Beck and Noah glanced at Dorin. Addi found it highly coincidental that each event seemed to be geared towards each guy's strength. If the point was to have a clear winner, why level the playing field?

Each man nodded to the Queen then returned to their plates. No one spoke after that, they ate in tense silence until her mother finally left.

Everyone let out a deep sigh once they were alone. "She is a lot of things, but I never thought her crazy. I'm starting to rethink that assessment."

Dorin pushed his plate away from him. "Honestly, we shouldn't be surprised. We knew this was a possibility, and the school tried to prepare us for all aspects of royal life, and that included being in *exceptional* physical condition.

A thought occurred to Addi. "You all don't seem as innocent as I am. Did your training include that?"

All three exchanged glances, no one wanted to be the one to speak up. Finally, Noah gave in. "Before we could return, we needed to know every aspect of pleasing the future Queen."

Addi crossed her arms in front of her. She didn't know why this was bothering her so much. She glanced around to make sure none of the staff had come in. "Let me be explicitly clear in what I am asking. Were you taught about sex and if so was it only in theory or in practice?"

The guys looked everywhere but at her. "Noah?" She knew he wouldn't be able to ignore her.

He dropped his shoulders in resignation. "We had to practice everything we were taught."

Addi was horrified.

All three men started speaking at the same time. She could hear their apologies and explanations about how it didn't mean anything to them. All she could hear was the blood rushing in her ears.

Noah came around the table and grabbed her chin and forced her to look at him. "We did what we had to do to get back to you. Please don't hate us."

Addi jerked up, her chair screeching across the floor. "I don't hate you, I don't blame any of you." She looked at each of them. "After everything they put you through they had to add insult to injury and treat you like whores. How do you not hate me?"

Dorin stood up and pulled her into a hug. "When will you realize we were made for you and we wouldn't want it any other way. We're not brainwashed, we had the opportunity to travel and have a lot of different experiences while we were at school. All of that means nothing, we played our parts while we counted the days to come back to you."

Beck walked over and ran his hand down her back. "We are well aware of the unique situation we're in, and none of us would change a thing."

Addi felt the tension leaving her body. She was surrounded by her three favorite people, and they were right. They were the fierce foursome, and her mother needed to back down and give them time to figure everything out. Eventually, she would know which one she loved most, and then he would be her King.

She stepped back and smiled at them. "Enough drama for one day, let's go meet your brothers and sisters."

Beck quirked an eyebrow at her. "Sixteen teenagers at a pool party and you think there won't be drama?

***

Addi went into the bathroom to change into her bathing suit. The smell of chlorine and food was an odd mixture. Marta had set up a huge buffet next to the pool. At least she was supportive, Addi knew she could always count on her.

She slipped on her skimpy bikini and smiled at herself in the mirror. Like everything else illicit in Addi's life, this had been smuggled in by Shawna. One day in a fit of annoyance over the granny suits she was forced to wear Shawna swore she was going to give Addi a suit that she could feel sexy in even if she never got to wear it anywhere but her bedroom. She had never dreamed she would actually get to wear it in front of other people. The red top crisscrossed under her breasts and tied around her back. The tighter the knot, the more her breasts were pushed up. She wasn't sure where the cleavage came from, it looked incredible. The bottoms were tied into tiny bows high on her hips. She loved how the cut made her legs look longer than they were.

She stared at herself in the mirror. "You got this, pretend you're confident, and others will believe it." Mrs. Parsons drilled that into her head almost daily.

She took a deep breath and walked back out to the table Shawna had been sitting at. All three guys had shown up while she was changing, and they stood there staring at her. She could feel their eyes all over her body. Her nipples instantly hardened, heat pooled between her legs. Maybe this was a bad idea after all.

She glanced over and saw Shawna watching the guys, she was laughing at their reactions.

The muscles in Dorin's neck were standing out. She realized this was the most skin he'd seen on her so far. They had been fully clothed when they kissed. That was definitely something she wanted to remedy.

She walked over to the buffet and grabbed a cherry. She glanced at each guy and smiled as she popped it in her mouth. Beck's jaw dropped slightly, she loved their reactions to her.

The spell was broken when the door to the pool house swung open. Dorin walked over to her and handed her a towel. "I don't want my brother's ogling you, any chance you want to cover up?"

She locked her arms around his neck and smiled up at him. "Your brothers can look all they want. I'm not interested in them. Besides, I would think you would want to make your brother's jealous seeing what you have, and they don't." She leaned up on her tippy toes and gave him a quick peck before spinning around and walking over to meet the stream of teens walking in.

Eleven

Addi's stomach was rolling, she was so nervous meeting kids her own age. Beck met his group at the door first and brought them over to her. "Addi, these are my brothers Charlie and Ben, and my sister's Chrissy and Angelina."

All four quickly bowed and curtsied, she could see they were as nervous as she was. "No need for formalities." She didn't want them treating her like the princess, plus the extra attention felt strange given her attire. "It's so nice to meet all of you."

She shook Charlie's hand first, she could see the resemblance. He had the same crystal-clear blue eyes as his brother, but he was shorter and stockier. Ben winked at her as he shook her hand, he had blonde hair and green eyes. His bone structure was similar. Beck must look like one of his parent's more and Ben more like the other. When she got to Chrissy and Angelina she gave them each a quick hug, they looked ready to pass out.

She waved her hand towards the buffet. "Help yourselves to lunch while we wait for everyone else to show up."

The group moved on, Noah stood waiting with his two sisters. Addi understood now what he was saying about one refusing to wear a dress. The two girls looked almost identical down to the smattering of freckles across their noses, but one was in a yellow one-piece bathing suit, and the other was in a black tank top and men's long bathing suit shorts. Her hair was cut short, while the others was braided down her back.

Noah pointed at the tomboy first. "Addi I would like you to meet Tye." Tye waved hello, Addi was surprised she showed no hint of nerves. It took a lot of nerve to buck tradition and social norms, Addi was in awe of the girl immediately. If only she had that kind of strength to stand up to her mother more.

Noah pointed to his other sister. "This is my other sister, Chloe."

The girl bounced up on her toes and squealed. "It is so great to meet you. You are so beautiful. I can't believe I'm talking to the Princess!" Addi laughed. Noah and Tye both covered their faces in embarrassment.

Addi held her arms out and caught the girl as she launched into her arms. "It's nice to meet you too."

Chloe leaned back and turned to Noah. "Okay, I get it now."

Addi gave him a questioning look, he shook his head and dragged his sisters towards the food. She glanced back towards the door, a shiver ran down her spine. Dorin stood there devouring her with his eyes. She loved that her bathing suit was affecting him so much.

He waved over his shoulder, and three giants followed behind him. Addi was shocked by how similar they all looked. If she didn't know better, she would assume he was a quadruplet. A brief image of four Dorin's pleasuring her had goosebumps popping up on her arms.

"Addi, I'd like you to meet William, James, and Parker." William bowed his head as he shook her hand. Dimples popped up on James' cheeks as he gave her a big grin.

Parker grabbed her hand, instead of shaking it, he leaned down and kissed the top of it. "It is definitely my pleasure to meet you."

Dorin grabbed him by the scruff of his neck and yanked him away, his other two brother's each took a turn smacking him on the back of the head. Addi couldn't help giggling at Dorin's display of jealousy.

The foursome walked off, which left Shawna, her brother, and sister. Both Jared and Suzanna were a little calmer about meeting the princess. They probably knew more about her than anyone else in the entire palace. Suzanna looked similar to Shawna except she didn't have the scarring on her face.

Addi walked with the group over to the buffet and made a plate. As she turned towards the tables, she paused, every pair of eyes were on her. Some were trying to be more covert than others, but they were definitely all watching her. She was used to it, and this was most definitely a new experience for all of them, so she didn't hold it against them.

She straightened her shoulders and took the seat at the head of the long table. She was glad the guys had thought to push all the tables into a rectangle so she wouldn't be forced to choose who she sat near.

For a few minutes, the silence was deafening, the only sound she heard was her own chewing. She cleared her throat and got everyone's attention. "I want to thank you all for coming and appeasing my curiosity. You can imagine how much I wanted to meet you all. I'm sure you're as wonderful as your brothers are." Addi ignored the snort from one of Dorin's brothers. I know this seems like a strange situation to all of you, so I want to make it clear I am an open book."

She ignored the shocked look from her trio of suitors. She knew it was a bold choice to bring up the elephant in the room.

Parker immediately raised his hand. "Now that you have seen us, any chance you want to swap one of us out?" He wiggled his eyebrows up and down.

Tye snorted. "That was smooth, Casanova."

Dorin glared at his brother. "I'm going to drown you."

Addi couldn't help laughing at their banter, at that moment she knew she would never stop at only one child. Everyone deserves siblings, even if you wanted to kill them sometimes. "I would say whoever wins the pool volleyball game can stay." Her three guys swung around and looked at her like she was insane. "However, none of this is up to me, and I know the Queen would not agree to that deal." Like she would ever trade any of them for someone else. Whether they liked it or not, they were hers, and she wasn't giving them up without a fight.

Twelve

Dorin wanted his brother gone. Parker had spent the entire afternoon hitting on Addi. He could see she loved every minute of it, so he let it slide, but it still annoyed the shit out of him. Beck, Noah, and Dorin had taken on the other six guys in volleyball and managed to beat them. If the other two were feeling like he was, they wanted to reassert their place with Addi and remind the boys not to get comfortable.

By the time the siblings were changed and packing up to leave, Dorin was itching to get his hands on her. He'd watched her breasts bouncing in the tiny string top for so many hours he was getting serious blue balls and needed relief. His ego needed a little pampering too, he wasn't going to admit he was pouty with how well she got along with his brothers.

He walked over to Beck and Noah. "I'd like to chat with Addi for a bit, think you can get Shawna out of here?"

Beck gave him a sardonic look. "Chat...yeah that's what I do with Addi too."

Dorin assumed the others had been testing the waters with Addi and it didn't bother him. If she was going to pick one of them, she needed to make sure they were compatible in all areas. Plus, she was a virgin. There was no way one of them was taking that step without a discussion between them first. He made a mental note to have that conversation sooner rather than later.

Noah patted his shoulder. "We got you, have fun and don't do anything we would do."

Dorin watched as Noah walked over to Shawna. "Hey, I heard you like to read. There are some fascinating books I want to show you."

Shawna looked confused but shrugged and followed him out of the pool house. Beck waved to Addi then chased after them.

Addi stood where Shawna left her, her cheeks were red. "Are you okay?"

She stared at the closed door with squinted eyes. "I'm trying to decide if I should kill Noah."

Dorin had no idea how books elicited such a response. He shrugged and let it go. "So, was today a good day?"

She turned back to him, a huge smile spreading across her face. "It was awesome, we have to do it again. It didn't really dawn on me how much I was missing out on until this." The smile fell from her face, she stared off in the distance for a few seconds. "I'm not just sheltered, I'm a prisoner. I've lost so many years of experiences because of my mother's controlling ways."

He wrapped his arms around her and inhaled her scent as she laid her head against his chest. "You're not even eighteen yet so you still have plenty of time. Plus, now that we're back we'll help you get caught up on life as a teenager. All four of us can sit down and make a bucket list of things you need to try or experience."

Her breath danced across his chest as she mumbled. "Can we take an item off the list right now?"

He stroked the soft skin of her back, his fingers tracing small circles across her shoulders. "Anything you want."

"Let me go down on you, and you can tell me what is right and wrong? I've read a lot, so I have a pretty good idea. I was thinking it would be better if you gave feedback while I'm doing it."

Dorin groaned, he hardened instantly at the idea of her mouth on him. *Let her* was not the right word, he should be the one to *beg her*. "You may be overestimating my abilities. I'm not sure how long I can stay coherent once you start touching me."

She pulled back to look up at him, a questioning look in her eyes.

"Unless you're trying to eat me like corn on the cob, it's going to feel good, and after a certain point, my brain is going to shut off. This is embarrassing to admit, I'll probably be a groaning, rutting mess, so I'm sure you will be able to tell I'm enjoying it." He smiled at her wide-eyed expression. "You are about to learn exactly how much control you have over me."

He grabbed her hand and pulled her over to the steps of the pool.

"You know I can't breathe underwater, right?"

"I don't think the pool deck is going to be good on your knees so I'll sit on the top step and you can float between my legs. Between the water, the steps, and using my legs to support you, it should be pretty comfortable."

She gave him a cheeky smile. "Was pool sex one of your assignments at school?"

She had to bring that up. "No, Ms. Smartypants." He stepped into the warm water and went all the way under. He came up for air as she swam the length of the pool. He sat on the top step, the water only going halfway up his thighs. He watched her effortlessly glide through the water as she came back and swam straight up to him. She popped up out of the water between his legs.

Her hands rested on the lower step, her arms pushed her breasts together, they strained against the triangles of cloth trying to hold them in. He was already going to lose the ability to talk before they'd even started. He cleared his throat, then leaned forward and kissed her. The sweet taste of her was a drug to him, his hands fisted in the wet strands of her hair. It was going to be a battle to not take control and get his mouth on more of her.

She finally broke free and pushed on his chest. "Lean back." Her fingers traced up his thighs until she reached the strings of his shorts. She pinched one string with her finger and thumb and pulled slowly, her eyes never broke contact with him. She took her time loosening the laces until she could pull the front down, freeing his painfully engorged dick.

Once he was free, she broke eye contact and looked down.

"Have you seen a cock before?" She shook her head but didn't say anything. "I think you should try out whatever you want. If you want pointers let me know."

She glanced up at him. "I thought I would know how to start. Now you have me picturing corn on the cob, so I'm all confused."

He threw his head back and laughed. "I'm sorry, let me help you. Start out like you're licking an ice cream cone then mix it up with sucking on a milkshake so thick you can't get anything up the straw. From there, you alternate how hard you lick and suck and whether you take it all in or just the head."

He was panting by the end, just the idea of her doing any of those things was making pre-cum dribble out.

She nodded and went back to studying his erection. He could see the wheels turning in her head, lord love her she was making a plan of attack, wasn't she?

"It really does bounce around a lot, doesn't it?"

He closed his eyes and tried not to laugh. He couldn't help the flexing it was doing, it was like a heat-seeking missile, and it knew her mouth was close. He chose to ignore the question instead.

He was about to beg her to touch him when she leaned forward and ran her tongue from the base to the tip. Her tongue curled around the shaft, the wet heat hugging him as she moved upwards.

He hadn't realized he was holding his breath until the burning in his chest made him gasp for air. He watched as she twisted and turned, licking and kissing from different angles. He wanted to grab her head and have her suck, but he knew this was about her learning not his pleasure.

She slowly slid her soft lips down his shaft, she moved up and down a few times without sucking. "Please."

Her throaty chuckle sent vibrations across his skin. After a few more passes, she latched on and sucked hard. He bucked against her, he hadn't meant to. The change of sensations was so drastic it surprised him.

She reached inside his shorts, her nails scraping across his balls. He definitely hadn't taught her that. If he didn't know her, he would never have believed she was innocent. Her mouth was exquisite, he wanted to put his hand around her neck and hold her while she drained him, but he knew that was too much for the first time.

His need to come was intensifying the more he watched her, she had her eyes closed, and she devoured him as if he were the best treat she'd ever eaten. Finally, he was toeing the line of finishing. "You can stop now and finish with your hand." Sometimes it sucked being a gentleman.

She pulled back and looked up at him, her forehead scrunched in confusion. "What? Why would I stop, you haven't finished?"

"I'm saving you from the surprise of my cum shooting down your throat. Most women don't enjoy that part."

She rolled her eyes. "I told you I know stuff. I've read enough to know what to expect. I won't know if I like it or not if I don't try it. So close your eyes and try to enjoy."

He snorted. "I don't have to try, you're amazing." He leaned forward and gave her a quick kiss before she pushed him back and went to what she was doing.

It didn't take long before he was bucking again, his hands lightly holding her head. She squeezed his balls just as he exploded inside her mouth. Lights danced across his vision, he collapsed back against the ground, gasping for air.

"Was that good?"

He could hear how unsure she was, but he didn't have much use of his brain yet, all he managed was his arm flopping into the air, and he gave her a thumbs up. He heard her chuckle then the water splash as she took off doing laps. How is she not exhausted, he sure was.

Every run-in he had with her had him dreading the day she chose one of them. Two of them were going to be devastated.

Thirteen

Addi sat at the dinner table, her nails lightly tapped on the table as she waited for the guys. The door swung open, her hand flew to her mouth, stifling a gasp. All three had a combination of busted lips, bloody noses, or black eyes. Their hair was disheveled, and they weren't making eye contact with her.

They went to their chairs and sat. The silence was deafening.

She caved first. "Well?"

Noah glanced up at her. "Evening Princess."

She crossed her arms across her chest. "Out with it."

Beck shrugged. "It's no big deal. We needed to work something out."

She scoffed at them. "Try again."

Dorin took a sip of water, wincing as the glass touched his swollen lip. "We were disagreeing on something but worked it out. It's handled now, and we can move on."

"If this was about me I'm going to be pissed."

All three looked down at their laps.

"Children...I'm dealing with children." She shook her head at them. "Next time something this obviously important comes up, and it involves me, how about asking how I feel about it?"

She waited for all three to nod before giving in and eating dinner. If they wanted to be idiots, she was not going to feel sorry for them when they got hurt.

She passed a bowl of potatoes then asked. "Is everyone ready for this stupid race tomorrow?" All three nodded. "I'm tempted to pick one of you just to save you from my mother's games."

Identical looks of fear stared back at her. Pain lanced through her chest, it hurt knowing they were as scared as she was about the looming choice. "Forget I said anything, let's eat and talk about anything not related to us or our situation."

Everyone readily agreed and dug into their food. This is the way she wanted it, just her and her three men.

***

Addi was a mess, she had barely slept. Her looming choice was weighing heavily on her. Knowing the first contest was today she had been up all night trying to decide if she could pick one of them first and save them all the trouble and risk. By the time the sun had come up, she was exhausted and no closer to making a choice.

She was dozing off when Shawna came in with a tray of food. "The race is going to start soon. I figured you would want to get down there quickly. The guys have already eaten and are down there looking over the horses."

Addi shot out of the chair, how had she not heard them leave their rooms? She threw on the first dress in the closet and grabbed a croissant off the tray as she ran out of the room and made her way to the barn.

As soon as she made it outside, she slowed to a fast walk and went into the barn. At first, it was silent then she heard voices outside. She followed the sounds and found all three guys looking over a line of horses. Niles walked with them and discussed each animal's pros and cons. Everyone turned and nodded to her, then went back to the task at hand. She wasn't surprised when Dorin chose Valliant. He was one of the strongest looking horses there. Beck chose another horse that was large and menacing looking. She chuckled when Noah walked over and nuzzled Deloris.

"Um, either you know something we don't know, or you are trying to fake us out." Dorin studied the small mare currently rubbing her nose against Noah's neck.

Beck agreed. "Yeah, he's a better horseman. If he picked her, I think we made poor choices."

Noah smiled cheekily. "Sorry boys, I did let you go first."

Before the bickering could escalate, the Queen walked to the fence line. Everyone immediately froze and went silent. "Are you ready to begin?"

All three men nodded then shocked Addi when they walked over to her, bowed and kissed her hand. Each one said the same thing. "I pledge myself to you." Her cheeks were red as they turned away and mounted their horses.

Addi glanced over and saw the Queen staring at her, a barely perceptible look of irritation on her face.

Niles waved to the group. "Line up over there, on the count of three you'll go. We've already discussed the route, first one back wins."

Addi's stomach dropped as they got in position. This was asinine and archaic. She turned her back on her mother and sat on the bench closest to the finish line.

Everything was silent except the three horses all tensing ready to go. It was as if they knew what was at stake.

Niles stood to the right of the trio. "On three gentlemen. One. Two. Three."

The horse's hooves thundered across the ground as all three took off. Addi chuckled as Noah and Deloris took the lead quickly. She lost sight of them as they entered the forest. She suddenly wished she had asked Shawna to sit with her, she wouldn't make that mistake next time. She needed someone to distract her and help keep her from crawling out of her own skin.

If she wasn't so well trained she would be chewing on her nails, instead she sat perfectly still, refusing to let her mother see her nerves.

When Addi didn't think her back could stay straight a second longer, the sound of hooves echoed out of the forest. Beck broke through the trees first with Dorin on his heels. Addi should have watched the finish line, but she was staring at the forest. Noah should have been the clear leader. As Beck and Dorin stopped at the line, they both jumped down and turned to watch the trees too. It made her feel good to know they did care about each other. After a few seconds, Deloris broke the tree line. Addi gasped to see she was alone, Noah was nowhere to be seen. Everyone jumped into motion at the same time. Niles and a few of the groomsmen jumped on the horses that hadn't been chosen while Beck and Dorin got back on their horses. They took off back the way they came.

Deloris stopped in front of Addi, she grabbed the reins to mount her when her mother's sharp tone stopped her. "That is not what a Princess does. Let the men handle it."

Rage rolled through Addi, but she bit her tongue. She had to choose her battles, and in all honesty, there probably wasn't much she could do to help out there anyways.

She handed the horse off to a waiting groomsman and instructed another to call for a doctor. The creaking of the barn doors had her glancing over to see one of the horses being walked out with a flat cart strapped to his saddle. She recognized the large supply bag in the back from when she had fallen. She knew they were cautious. It scared her to think they may need it.

Addi paced the field, she was about to grab a horse and take off when the group came into view. Dorin and Beck raced ahead of the cart. They rode up to Addi and jumped off the animals before they had even fully stopped.

Beck grabbed her arms. "He's okay, he was thrown and hit a tree. He's not awake, but he seems okay. Did anyone call for a doctor?"

She nodded, unable to get any words out.

Dorin tossed the reins of both horses to a groomsman and turned to Addi. "Let's get up to the house, they are going to pull the cart right up to the door."

She wanted to lean on them, but her mother was watching. She pushed her shoulders back and marched past her.

Doctor Hamil was standing at the back door to the kitchen waiting. He listened as Beck and Dorin detailed out what they saw. They didn't have a lot of detail as they let Niles feel for injuries, so the group waited as the cart was rolled slowly across the field. She took comfort that they would be going much faster if he were critical.

Nausea was threatening to overcome Addi as the cart pulled up, and she saw Noah covered in mud, and what she assumed was blood. They had put one of his arms in a splint and gauze was taped in a few areas. Tears burned her eyes, but she blinked them away.

Dr. Hamil strode up to the cart. "Let me check him over before you move him." He methodically checked his eyes, neck, and back. "I can call for a stretcher to be brought over, but I think it's safe for him to be carefully carried inside."

Marta came out of the door, worry etched across her face. "I have blankets being brought down. You can use them to carry him in." She grabbed Addi's hand and squeezed. "Let's get out of the way, you can help me get his room ready."

Grateful to have something to keep her busy Addi followed her upstairs. A nurse was already up there setting out supplies. Addi grabbed the blanket from his bed and pulled it back. His scent hit her, goosebumps danced along her arms.

As she heard voices coming down the hall, she stepped back and moved out of the way. Dorin, Beck, and three groomsmen carried Noah in. They set him in bed and moved so the doctor and nurse could take over.

Beck and Dorin walked over and stood by her. She didn't care who was in the room; she wrapped an arm around each one's waist and pulled them against her. She needed their comfort, and not even her mother could pry her away from them at that moment.

They stood in silence, one rubbing her back while the other's hand massaged her neck. They watched as their friend, her love, was poked, prodded, and bandaged.

A while later, Dr. Hamil finally stepped back and walked over to them. "I think he's going to be fine. He should wake up soon, but he has a pretty large contusion on his head. His pupils are normal and reactive, so I don't think we need to worry about any bleeding. He has a couple of bruised ribs and a lot of scrapes. I don't think anything is broken though. I don't want him having anything stronger than Tylenol, and once he wakes up, you can let him nap again, but I want him woken up once an hour."

"Doctor, he's waking up." The nurse stepped aside as their group rushed to the bed. They held their breath as he blinked his eyes a couple of times then focused them on Addi. "What are you doing in my room?" He glanced around, his eyebrows were drawn together in confusion.

Dr. Hamil cleared his throat. "You were thrown from your horse. Is anything hurting?"

Noah stared at him for a second before answering. "Pretty much everything hurts but nothing I can't handle." He looked at Beck and Dorin. "I was thrown?"

Dorin and Beck glanced at each other before Dorin answered. "We didn't actually see what happened. When you made the turn to come back, something spooked your horse, and you started fighting for control. We took off ahead of you never thinking you would get knocked off."

Dr. Hamil held Noah's wrist as he took his pulse. "Give it time, and you'll start to remember what happened. Now I want you to rest, I've already told them to wake you hourly." He turned to the trio. "Call if anything changes, otherwise I'll be back in the morning to check on him."

As he and his nurse were leaving Marta and a couple of the groomsmen came in. She was carrying a large tray of food, and they had chairs. "I assume you will want to take your meal in here so you all should at least be comfortable." She set the tray on the table in the corner and walked over to Noah. "I brought you soup, nothing heavy for you right now." She brushed the hair from his forehead then left. Addi could see the tears in her eyes.

Once the foursome was alone, they pulled the table by the bed. Addi grabbed the soup bowl, but Noah held his hand up. "Nothing for me right now, I just need to sleep." His eyes fluttered closed.

They ate in silence and watched him. The food in Addi's stomach didn't sit well. Noah was an expert rider, was it really an accident or was her mother somehow involved?

Fourteen

Beck finished his shower and went back to Noah's room. Addi was curled up in a chair asleep. Both he and Dorin had taken breaks throughout the evening, but she never left Noah's side.

Dorin came in right behind him. "How about I take the night watch, you try to get her to take a break? She needs to sleep in a normal bed."

"I don't know if she'll leave but let's try."

They walked over, Beck lightly nudged her shoulder. "Addi, wake up?"

Her eyes fluttered open, she looked alarmed. "Is he okay?"

Dorin held his hand up to stop her. "He's fine, but you aren't. I don't want you in this chair any longer. I'm going to stay with Noah, and you are going to bed."

She tried to shake her head, but Noah woke up and interrupted them. "Addi go to bed, I'm fine."

She walked over and grabbed his hand. "You must have hit your head harder than I thought. You are sending me away?"

He chuckled at her. "When I'm back on my feet tomorrow I will show you how much I want you with me. Until then, you need your rest." He looked around her at Beck. "Please force her to go to bed."

Beck nodded and rested his hand on her back. "Come on, it's late."

She leaned down and kissed Noah's cheek then followed Beck out the door. They stopped at her bedroom door. He tucked a lock of hair behind her ear. "Do you need anything?"

She bit her lip as she glanced up and down the hall. "I don't want to be alone, will you lay with me until I fall asleep?"

Beck thought that sounded like torture, but he was willing to give her whatever she needed. "After you." He pushed her door open.

She walked in and went straight to her dresser. "I'm going to change, I'll be right back."

He walked around her room, looking at the small details that had changed over the years while they were gone. Instead of figurines of animals, she had glass perfume bottles and pretty jewelry boxes. This was definitely not the little girl he left behind.

She came back wearing a satin tank top and shorts. The peach color looked good against her auburn hair. "Ready?"

Beck really wished she was a little more precise with her question. He was ready to do so many things with her. He settled for nodding and letting her lead.

Her hands were twisted together nervously as she walked over and pulled back her blanket. She got in and patted the space next to her.

He laid down and held his arm out, she immediately rolled into his side. "Would you mind taking your shirt off?"

He prayed she asked him to strip more, he was tensely trying to control his need for her, but he wanted her relaxed. "You're not planning to take advantage of me, are you? I promised I would make you sleep."

She shrugged. "If something happens and we work hard enough at it I'm sure I'll sleep well after."

His jaw dropped open, did she really mean what he thought she did? He leaned up and ripped his shirt off and tossed it on the floor. She curled against him again and lightly stroked her fingers across his stomach. "Will you tell me what the fight was about last night?"

Oh, she's good. She knew how to catch him off guard. He contemplated what to tell her and opted to go with the truth. "Are you sure you want to know? You might not be too happy with us."

"Well, now I have to know. You are making it sound too juicy for me to ignore."

"Um..." he cleared his throat, "you see, we were working out who would get to um..."

He felt stupid. The words sounded ridiculous to him, so he knew how it would sound out loud.

"You fought over who was going to take my virginity?"

He froze, how did she know? "More like, *if* it were to happen, who should get to sleep with you first. No one planned to take anything from you."

She shook her head. "By the damage done, I'm not sure if I can tell which one of you won."

"Who did you want to win?" He knew it wasn't a fair question, deep down, he really wanted to know.

Her head popped up, she glared at him. "I don't think so, you know I love you all and asking me to choose between you for anything is the last thing I want to do right now. I'm tired of having to think about which one of you is going to be chosen. Please tell me which of you won."

"There's a reason Dorin took the night shift, it was so I could spend time with you."

She glanced up at him. "And now you're here to claim your prize?"

He shook his head. "Don't make it sound like you're on an object, that is not what any of that was about."

"What if I want you to claim me?"

He stared into her eyes, hoping she meant what she said. He pushed her back and rolled onto his side. "Close your eyes." He gently traced her face, then moved down to the dip in her throat. He could feel the flutter of her heartbeat. Her nipples were pushing against the fabric of her shirt, he drew small circles around one then the other.

Her breathing sped up, he smiled as she arched her back, he knew she wanted more. He left her shirt down but leaned over and flicked the tiny bud. He chuckled at her frustrated moan. After a few more teasing circles, he closed his mouth over it and sucked. Her hands fisted in his hair as she curled her back up to hold him closer.

He reached down, his hand sliding under the waistband of her shorts. As soon as his fingertips got to her clit, he could feel she was wet and ready. He already knew how she liked to be finger fucked, so he took her to the edge of an orgasm before stopping and rolling off the bed.

She gasped. "Where are you going? Now is not the time to leave me."

He laughed at her pout. "Relax, I'm just getting undressed." In one fluid motion, the rest of his clothes were off. He grabbed a condom out of the pocket of his pants then tossed them on top of his shirt. "Now it's your turn."

She sat up and pulled her shirt off then leaned back and slid her shorts off then laid back down with her knees bent and her legs spread. "Come back to me."

He didn't have to be asked twice. He climbed in bed and kneeled between her legs. "Are you ready?" She nodded, he could see the desire in her eyes.

He slipped the condom on then laid on top of her. For a few seconds, they laid still, both enjoying what the other felt like against them. He kissed her neck as he pushed his dick against her clit. He continued to grind against her until she was close again then he kissed her at the same time he slid inside her a couple of inches.

He slid in and out a few times, each stroke going a little deeper. She broke the kiss when the pain hit from him fully impaling himself. He stopped moving. "Are you okay?"

"Yeah, it was just a surprise. I didn't think women actually felt any pain, I thought it was a story used to scare girls into staying virgins."

"I'll stay still until you're ready."

She reached down, her hands cupping his ass. "Oh, I'm ready. It was only a little pinch. Show me what all the hype is about."

"So, no pressure...just make it good?"

She nodded and tilted her hips pushing against him. He never would have expected her to be so playful.

He leaned down and kissed her again, he pulled out and slowly slid back in. It was the sweetest torture to go slow. She must have felt the same way, after a few strokes her nails dug into his back. They settled into a rhythm, sweat broke out across his forehead, he was close. He wanted her to finish first. He pushed against her clit until she yelled out. Her body tensed as she came, he let himself go and finished with her.

After a few minutes of labored breathing, he pulled out and rolled off of her. She curled into his arms.

He contemplated what to say next. "So, is the hype worth it?"

She chuckled. "I think I get it, but I may have to try a few more times before I'm sure."

He didn't mean to laugh loudly. It burst out of him. "God, I love you."

She pushed back and looked up at him. "I love you too."

He studied her, did she love him enough to choose him? Did he just make the biggest mistake of his life by sleeping with her? She was now a part of him, and if he was sent away, he wasn't sure he would recover.

Fifteen

Addi sat in front of the mirror, looking at herself. Did she look any different? If someone looked at her, could they tell she had lost her virginity the night before?

Shawna walked over with a dress from the closet. "Marta said Noah was looking good this morning when she dropped his breakfast off. I still can't believe he got hurt."

Apparently, there wasn't a flashing neon sign over her head saying *Just Fucked*. Eventually, she would tell her best friend, but not yet.

"I find it hard to believe too. I've seen him ride, he is probably the best rider I've seen."

Shawna ran her fingers through Addi's hair, getting ready to braid it. "What did the Queen have to say? Is she calling off the rest of the challenges?"

Addi shrugged. "I've not seen her. Although I highly doubt she would call this off." She squirmed in her seat, she wanted to check on Noah before going down to breakfast.

Shawna finished her hair and stepped back. "Okay, you're ready to go."

Addi popped up and made her way to the room next door. She knocked gently and poked her head inside and found Dorin snoozing in the same chair she had slept in yesterday.

She walked in quietly and stood over Noah, she still couldn't believe he had gotten hurt.

"You're staring at me."

Noah's eyes fluttered open, and he smiled up at her.

She sat on the edge of the bed. "How are you feeling?" She reached up and brushed the hair back from his forehead.

"Good as new, I'm ready for today's trial."

Addi bolted to her feet. "Excuse me? There is no way you are doing a trial today."

Dorin jerked awake at her shout.

Noah sat up against the headboard. "You don't understand, I don't have a choice."

Dorin stood next to Addi and rested one hand on her shoulder. "He's right. The Queen sent a message that he had to compete, or he would be deemed unfit for the position and be sent home."

She shook her head, rage boiling inside her. "Absolutely not, this is ridiculous."

Addi stormed out of the room and went straight to her mother's suite. She was expected to knock, but she was too irate for that. She stormed inside, Liza jumped in alarm.

"Where is she?" Addi's nails dug into her palms.

"I'm right here." Her mother walked out of the adjoining room and gave her a frosty stare. "Is there something amiss?"

"How dare you say Noah has to compete today. Surely Dr. Hamil will agree he shouldn't be out of bed so soon."

"The point of the trials is to find the strongest man, both mentally, and physically, to be your husband. If he can't take a couple of bruises, then he is too weak to be considered."

Addi shook her head. "You've gone mad."

"Watch yourself dear, or I will forego the contest and choose for you." Addi hated seeing the look of triumph in her mother's eyes. "I suggest you get breakfast then make your way to the cliffs.

Addi spun on her heel and stormed out, she needed food and Shawna if she was going to get through the day.

*****

The wind was blowing Addi's hair in her face as she stood at the bottom of the cliffs. The water behind them was relatively calm, the exact opposite of what she was feeling.

The Queen was sitting on her horse, watching over everyone as the guys were hooked up to harnesses. Noah was pale and sweating, Addi wanted to stop the madness, but she knew she was forced to play her mother's game.

Queen Ellena rode forward. "The rules are simple, the first one to the top wins. Good luck, gentlemen."

Before they got in place, Addi walked over and kissed each one on the cheek. Noah was the last, she hugged him too. "I wish you wouldn't do this."

He squeezed her into a tight embrace. "You're worth it, have faith in me."

She walked back over and held Shawna's hand.

Niles stood next to the group. "Belayer's ready?"

Shawna leaned over and whispered. "What's a Belayer?"

Addi shrugged. "I think it's the three guys that stay on the ground and help control the ropes."

Niles continued. "On three. One... Two... Three."

It was silent except for the waves behind them as the three guys started their accent. Beck took a quick lead, Dorin was right on his heels. Poor Noah was going the slow and steady route, but Addi was relieved he was making progress.

By the time they were three-quarters of the way from the top Beck had taken a sizeable lead. He reached his right hand up when he yelled out and started falling backward. Addi screamed as she saw his rope had broken, and he was free-falling.

Everything happened in seconds. Dorin pushed off the wall and caught Beck's hand. The extra weight caused them both to fall a few feet before the belayers were able to help slow them down. They reached for the walls and found their footing again.

Addi wanted them to come down and stop the madness, instead, they started going back up. It was a moot point though, her turtle, Noah was at the top climbing over the edge.

She waited until the other two were safely to the top before she and Shawna got on their horses and rode to the top. Noah was standing proudly, his smile taking up half his face. She gave him a thumbs-up before walking over to check on Beck and Dorin. Both were sitting on the ground, breathing heavily.

"Are you both okay? You scared me."

Beck glanced up at her. "Scared me too. I was sure I was a goner."

Dorin groaned as he stood up. "I would never have let that happen. We have to stick together, right?" He held his hand out and helped Beck up.

That's when she saw the gashes down his right side. She reached out and pulled his shirt up where a large amount of blood was spreading.

"When Dorin caught me, I slammed against the wall, it's a few minor cuts. We'll tape them up and be fine."

She glanced at the gash on his side. "I think you may need stitches, I'll send for Dr. Hamil just to be safe."

Niles had been prepared and pulled up with the flat cart and medical supply bag. "Let's get you bandaged up until the doc gets here."

Addi walked over to Noah. "Congratulations." She gave him a hug. "Are you okay?"

"Every part of my body hurts, and my head is throbbing, but I finished. Your mom can take that and shove it up her..." He took a deep breath and shook his head. "Anyways, if you don't mind, I'm going back to bed until the trial tomorrow."

He climbed on his horse and left. After quite a bit of arguing, Beck agreed to ride in the cart. When they made it back, he refused help and walked himself up to his room where Dr. Hamil was already waiting.

He shook his head as he took in the bloody bandages. "Are you going to be doing a lot of high-risk activities around here? Maybe I should plan to visit every day?"

Beck pulled his torn shirt off and tossed it near the garbage can. "The worst one is tomorrow then I think we're done."

Dr. Hamil turned and looked at Addi in outrage. "You can't put these boys through this, it isn't right."

Addi held her hands up. "It's not my doing, I've begged the Queen, but she insists on one more." *Unless I give in and choose one of the guys first.*

He closed his mouth and turned back to Beck. He knew he had no say in what the Queen dictated.

The group sat silently until he finished his work and left. Dorin broke the silence first. "Did you see the way the rope was broken?"

Beck nodded grimly.

Addi was confused. "What am I missing?"

Dorin let out a heavy sigh. "It didn't look like it broke as much as it was cut."

Addi gasped. "You think the belayer cut the rope?"

Beck shook his head. "I'm not saying he did it. Someone could have cut it most of the way and let it snap during the race or anyone on that beach could have done it before we started."

Addi knew who was behind it. "It's my mother, she is pissed I'm not choosing so she's trying to speed things along by taking you guys out of the equation."

Dorin and Beck both stared at her in shock. "That is a heavy accusation, Addi."

She paced the room. "I know I have no proof, but I believe it with every fiber of my being. You guys need to be careful tomorrow. I don't see how she could cause an issue with the hand to hand combat, but if there is, she will find a way."

Beck laid back against the pillows. "I guess I better get my rest if I want any chance of beating you."

Dorin laughed. "Don't worry, I won't purposely aim for any of your injuries."

Addi was horrified they could talk so casually about fighting each other. "You guys are ridiculous. I'm going to check on Noah."

She spun on her heel and left them. Noah was her gentle giant, she knew he would help her forget about the impending fight.

Sixteen

Noah stared up at the ceiling. He still couldn't believe he'd won. The other two should have been able to climb up and repel down before he had even made it to the top, Beck's accident was his lucky break.

What was plaguing him was whether it was a coincidence both of them were hurt or if there was something else going on.

A soft knock interrupted his musing. "Come in."

Addi walked in. "Want some company?"

He didn't care how much he hurt, he wasn't sending her away again. "I always want your company."

She walked to the edge of the bed. "Mind if I lay next to you?"

He pulled back the covers, her eyes widened when she glanced down at him. He only had on a pair of basketball shorts. "I can put a shirt on if you'd like?"

She shook her head and climbed in next to him. "Nope, I'm good."

He laughed at her eagerness. "So, how are you handling all of this?"

She let out a heavy sigh. "I'm tired of the drama of my mother, of the choice. I just want to relax and have fun with you guys."

He had ideas of how to have fun, but he didn't know what she was thinking. "I can accommodate that, what did you have in mind?"

Instead of speaking, she leaned up on one arm and got close to his face. Their breath mingled, her hand stroked his chest. She bent down and kissed him. He grabbed her neck and held her close. At first, they were slow and sensual then built until both were breathing heavy, and hands were roaming.

She pulled away and sat up, her back to him. "I can't do this."

He blinked a couple of times to clear the fog clouding his mind. "It's okay, we don't need to do anything."

She looked over her shoulder at him, her eyebrows squished together. "What? No, I mean I can't do anything with this stupid dress on. I can't move my legs at all. Can you undo the zipper for me?"

He bit back a moan of pain as he sat up and did as she asked. She stood and slid it down over her hips. She walked to the bedroom door and locked it. As she walked back, she unclipped her bra and tossed it aside. She stopped next to the bed and slid her underwear off before climbing back in next to him. "This is much better."

He had no words, maybe the concussion was worse than he thought. He had to be imagining this.

She swung one leg over him and straddled his thighs. Her pussy rested on the base of his erection. "Sweet Jesus, you are beautiful."

She smiled. "Teach me how to be in control?"

His breath lodged in his throat, she was going to kill him. "Well, it really isn't hard. Men are simple, stupid creatures, and you really do hold all the power over us." She laughed, but he was serious. "You can tease me by not letting me touch you, and you do it yourself. When you're on top, you can control the speed and if it's sensual or aggressive."

"Do you have any condoms?"

He pointed toward the nightstand. "We were well supplied when we moved back."

She shook her head as she leaned over and grabbed one out of the drawer. He watched as she ripped it open and held the circular object as she inspected it.

"Put it over the head, leaving a little room at the tip then roll it down." Lucky for both of them he was rock hard, so she had something to work with immediately.

She grabbed his dick and stroked it slowly. "I love how warm it is."

No one had ever said that to him. "Um, thank you?"

She shrugged. "Just an observation." She scraped her nails across his balls, he had no control over his body as his eyes closed, and moaned loudly.

She continued to torture him until he was panting and begging. "Please, I need more."

Her hand left him and slid up her stomach to her breasts. She took one in each hand; her fingers squeezed her nipples. Her head fell back as she moaned. She rocked against his dick, he was going to come right then if he didn't get control. This was what he had been fantasizing about for years. Every time he practiced something, he imagined it was her, and now it really was.

She looked down at him, her eyes clouded with lust. She slid the condom on his throbbing cock. "What now?"

"Just go up on your knees and guide me inside."

He wasn't surprised she was a quick learner. She reached between her legs and moved him so he was lined up. She slowly lowered herself. He stayed perfectly still, she needed time to adjust. Once he was buried inside her balls deep, she squeezed the muscles surrounding him.

"Where'd you learn that?"

She shrugged. "It just felt right."

"By all means, if it feels right keep going."

He reached up with both hands and cupped her breasts, his thumbs stroking her nipples. "Find your rhythm."

She leaned up and slid down again. After a few more strokes, she started increasing her speed. Her breasts were bouncing as she rode him. She had never looked hotter than in that moment. Once he felt the orgasm coming, he reached down with this thumb and rubbed her clit. He felt her muscles contract again right before she yelled out her own orgasm. As she was coming down, he let go and came.

She collapsed down on top of him, her hair covering his face. Their sweat running together as she panted against him.

He moved her hair then laid there stroking her back until she had calmed down. "That was mind-blowing, you were beautiful to watch."

She shook her head against his chest. "I don't even want to know what my face looks like at the end there."

"I personally love your wounded animal look."

He laughed as she pinched his side. "Way to flatter a girl."

"I figure I've already told you I love you and that you're beautiful, so I thought maybe I needed to put your ego in check. We don't want our princess getting too high and mighty, do we?"

She glanced up and gave him a quick kiss. "You're lucky I love you or I would take offense."

His breath caught in his chest. This was the most perfect moment of his life, and he had no idea if there would ever be another one with her. Could he make this memory last until his dying day?

Seventeen

Day three of the contests, Addi wasn't sure she had it in her to watch anymore. Maybe if she stayed in bed, her mother would postpone the last one.

Shawna came in and pulled back the curtains. "Good morning."

Addi groaned and tossed a pillow over her face. She felt the bed move as Shawna sat down and poked her. "What's up with you?"

Addi mumbled from under the pillow. "The last couple of days have been very physically demanding."

The pillow was ripped from her face. "I think I know what you are saying, but you aren't saying anything so spill the beans right this second."

She bit her lip, trying not to giggle. "Let's just say I've taken two of the guys for a test run."

Shawna squealed and hit her with the pillow. "Oh my god, look at you sleeping with two of them, why not the third?"

Addi rolled her eyes. "I'm pacing myself, I think for a beginner one a day is a good pace, don't you?"

Shawna shrugged. "I guess you're right. So, which two did you do the dirty with?"

It felt awkward talking about them, but she was dying to. "First was Beck and then yesterday was Noah."

Shawna's eyes sparkled with excitement. "How did you decide which one to do first?"

Addi hugged the pillow against her chest. "It wasn't planned, it just kind of happened with Beck and then with Noah he was laying there, so I decided to see where it went."

"So, which was better?"

Addi glared at her. "Really, what kind of question is that."

Shawna held her hands up defensively. "An honest one, most women would want to know."

Addi thought about it for a second. "They were so different, I'm not sure I can say. With Beck, he was patient and loving and made sure my first

158

time was good. With Noah, he showed me how to take control and do what felt good to me."

Shawna fanned herself. "I have never been more jealous of you than I am right now. Now the question is when are you going to do Dorin?"

"I think we need to get through the third contest then see what happens. I'm not planning anything, just doing what feels right."

Shawna stood up from the bed. "If it were me, I would be in his room right now giving him a good luck fuck, but you do you girl."

Her friend walked to the closet and pulled out a dress.

As fun as the idea sounded, she didn't want to distract him before the contest. She groaned and got out of bed. The day was not going to wait for her.

***

Addi and Shawna walked out the back of the castle and over to the guard's housing. They had a work out area behind the building where the fighting was going to take place.

As they rounded the corner, they stopped in surprise. The other two contests had been somewhat private, this one was different. The soldiers were standing around in a large circle with the guys and Niles in the center.

Her mother walked up behind her. "How are you this morning, dear?"

Addi glanced over, then back at the crowd. "Nothing has changed, I'm still against these games."

"So, you have chosen?"

Addi refused to answer the question.

Her mother stepped forward and spoke over her shoulder. "As I thought."

The crowd parted to let them walk to the center. Everyone bowed to the Queen, her trio nodded to her.

Niles waved his hand in the air to get everyone's attention. "This is the final challenge. The Queen feels you wouldn't try very hard if you faced off against each other. Instead, you will go against her best guards."

This surprised Addi, she would have thought the Queen would love to have them beat each other until only one was left standing.

Niles continued. "Beck, you will fight Daniel." A guard stepped forward Addi didn't recognize. He was similarly built to Beck but covered in scars. "Noah will fight Stephan." He waved over another guard, he was shorter than Noah, but he was twice as wide as him. Addi prayed that wasn't all muscle. "Dorin, you will fight Tomas."

Murmurs broke out around the crowd, even Addi knew who Tomas was. The man was in his thirties, almost seven feet tall and tree trunks for arms and legs. He was a giant, it was completely unfair to put anyone against him.

Tomas walked over and stood in front of Dorin who had to look up at him. It was probably the first time in his life he'd ever needed to do that.

Niles held out a hat. "Inside are three numbers, this will determine who goes first."

All three men reached in and pulled a piece of paper out. They looked at each other then opened them at the same time. Niles glanced at the papers, then called out. "Dorin will go first, followed by Noah then Beck."

The circle expanded, everyone stepped back, leaving Tomas and Dorin in the center. Noah and Beck came over, and each stood on one side of her. She held their hands and prayed for Dorin's safety.

The two giants circled each other a few times before Dorin moved in. He wrapped his arms around the bigger man and lifted him off the ground. He attempted to throw him down, Tomas broke free.

Fists flew as they both tried to make contact with the other. Dorin broke Tomas's nose, blood ran down his face. Dorin's eye swelled shut from a hit he didn't block in time. The crowd was cheering, Addi stayed perfectly silent. She hated watching but knew she couldn't walk away.

Dorin got Tomas in a headlock, he kicked one leg out and threw the man down. Dorin landed on top and tried to keep him pinned. Tomas roared as he bucked and flipped their positions. Tomas had the advantage of size, he laid on top of Dorin smothering him. Addi could see Dorin's face, it was purple as he fought for air. She couldn't do it any longer. She ran to the center of the ring and screamed for everyone to stop. Tomas immediately got up and bowed.

Addi turned to her mother. "I'm done with this. The ball is in two days, you will have your decision then. No more contests." She reached down and helped Dorin up. With Beck and Noah at her side, the foursome walked back to the house. She didn't care that she had challenged her mother in front of everyone. She wasn't going to play her game any longer. It was time she faced the truth and pick who her future husband was going to be.

Eighteen

Dorin's lungs were burning. He had been seconds from losing consciousness when Addi stopped the fight. He didn't care how that looked to anyone else, he only cared what she thought. "I'm sorry Addi, I tried to win for you."

She rolled her eyes. "Let's get you to your room then we'll talk."

Beck and Noah left them at his door, they understood he needed to know where he stood with Addi.

Dorin kicked off his shoes and flopped across his bed. "Am I disqualified?"

Addi sat on the bed and curled her legs underneath her. "Don't be stupid, there was never any competition with me. I don't care who won any of the contests."

Dorin appreciated the sentiment, but she wasn't the one in charge of their fate at the moment. "Do you think the Queen will send me home for not finishing?"

"I would like to see her try. No one is going home until after my ball."

Someone would be going home though. Dorin didn't say it out loud, they both knew it. "Have you made your decision yet?"

She shook her head. "Well...I've not finished exploring all my options." Her hand went under his shirt, her fingers stroking the skin above his waistband.

"Have you explored with the other two yet?" He was pretty sure he knew the answer but still wanted to hear it.

She glanced up at him, her cheeks pink with embarrassment. "Will it upset you to know that I have?"

He rubbed his thumb along her bottom lip. "I know they love you as much as I do and we all offer something different to you, so I'm not jealous of them. Plus, I knew what was going to happen before we came back. I've had plenty of time to accept the situation."

"You make it sound so perfunctory."

His hand wrapped around her neck, he pulled her face close to his. "There is nothing perfunctory about what I want to do to you." He smiled as her breathing sped up. "Tell me how the other two fucked you."

He was taking a risk by talking dominantly to her, but he had a feeling she was going to like it.

Her tongue darted out and licked her bottom lip. "Beck was on top of me, and I was on top of Noah."

He nodded. "I think you need something a little hotter, stand up."

She smiled wide as she hopped off the bed. He turned so he was sitting on the edge and pulled her between his legs. He grabbed the bottom of her dress and pulled it up. His fingers slid up her thigh until they found her pussy. He rubbed her clit over her panties, her head rolled back as she moaned. "You're already wet for me, I like that."

Her nails dug into his shoulders as she steadied herself. He moved her panties to the side and slid two fingers inside. The wet, heat had him straining against his pants. He wanted to be buried deep in her so badly it hurt. "Pull one of your breasts out the top of your dress."

She let go of his shoulders and reached down her cleavage to bring one plump breast out. Her nipple was hard, the rigid lines calling to him. He latched on and sucked while he fingered her. She took it until her knees started going weak then he pulled out.

He stood up and moved out of the way. "Pull your dress up to your knees and get on your hands and knees on the bed."

She looked at him curiously for a second before doing as instructed. He bunched her skirt up so it was over her lower back. "That is a beautiful ass." He grabbed her hips and ground his cock against her, he wanted her to know how badly he wanted to fuck her.

"Please come inside me, I need you."

He loved to hear her beg. He grabbed a condom from the drawer and undid his pants. He freed his erection and put on the condom. "Are you ready for me?"

Her fists balled into the sheets. "Oh god, yes."

He moved her underwear aside and slid in slowly. He reached forward putting a hand on each shoulder and pulled her back against him. He couldn't get deeper if he tried. "So tight." he gasped from straining to go slow when all he wanted to do was pound her hard and fast.

Addi glanced over her shoulder at him. "Take me."

She was perfection.

He slid out and in again. Each time going a little harder, a little deeper. He reached around and grabbed her bouncing tits and squeezed her nipples. He slammed into her over and over until finally, he felt her tightening as she orgasmed. He thrust a few more times, then came with her.

Once he was spent, he pulled out, then collapsed onto the bed on his side with her pulled against him. They laid there for a while coming down from the high. "Are you okay?" He managed to mumble.

She twisted around to face him. "That was incredible."

He smiled a big, toothy grin. "Better than the other two?"

She quirked an eyebrow but refused to answer.

"I'm going to take your silence as confirmation." Before she could argue, he kissed her.

He laid back and pulled her close. The next few days were going to be torture waiting to find out what Addi was going to do.

Nineteen

The sun was peeking through the curtains, but Addi didn't want to get up. She had been up all night thinking about the guys and who she would choose. She didn't want her mother deciding, so it was up to her.

Shawna came in humming but stopped when she caught sight of Addi's face. "You look like crap, what happened?"

Addi glared at her. "Nothing much, just tormenting myself over what I'm going to do."

Shawna walked over and sat on the side of the bed. "Did you get alone time with Dorin?"

Addi couldn't help the smile that spread across her face. "Yes, and he was spectacular. They all are amazing, and that's my problem."

"From the outside, it seems like a good problem to have. I know you don't want to hurt any of them. This may be one of the few times I'm glad I'm just a normal girl."

Addi sat straight up. "You're right. If I weren't the Princess, I wouldn't have to worry about this.

I bet the guys would help me leave. I don't know where we'd go, but between us, we can figure it out."

Shawna bolted off the bed. "Addi, no, that's not the answer. You can't run away."

Addi stood up and grabbed the other girl's hands. "My mother is still young. She could remarry and have another heir. I would rather be hidden away somewhere with the guys then living this boring existence with just one of them."

"If you ask me to help, I will but let's think of another way."

Addi waved her off and started pacing the room. Now that the idea was in her head, it was all she could think about. The idea of freedom to do what she wanted, when she wanted was thrilling. She could dress however she'd like and have a cell phone. A long list of everything she would gain was rolling through her head when her door opened. All three guys tumbled through at the same time.

She glanced at them curiously. "Is everything alright?" She didn't care that she was still in her tank top and shorts either, all of them had already seen every bit of her, so she had nothing to hide.

Dorin strode forward. "Shawna came and got us."

Beck closed the door and walked towards her. "You can't be serious about leaving, you're the Princess."

Noah chimed in. "If we're the problem, let us make the decision for you. Two of us will willingly leave if it will make it easier on you."

Addi could see the pain those words caused him. To her, it was like a knife to her stomach. "I don't know another way. Don't you see, I want all of you. I can't choose, I can't lose two of you."

Dorin pulled her against him as the tears rolled down her face.

She sniffled. "This is tearing me apart, and I don't want to do it any longer. Can't we run away and be together, all of us?" She pulled back to look at them. She didn't know how they were going to react to her idea.

The three of them exchanged surprised looks. Beck turned back to her. "You want to live with all of us?"

She shrugged. "It sounds right. I love all of you, I want all of you, so why choose? Why can't I keep all of you?"

They stood silently, contemplating her words.

Dorin ran his hands through his hair. "It's just not done. What if we did runaway together and got a house. How would you feel if you were shunned? You wouldn't be the Princess any longer. People can be mean, and you've spent most of your life sheltered from that."

Beck nodded in agreement. "Not to mention the logistics of how we would live together with you. Would children be involved?"

Addi paused, she hadn't considered any of that, especially kids. "I don't know how it will work, but we love each other so we can make it work."

Noah held his hand up. "Question for you. Once you're Queen, you can change the rules. Why not pick one of us, then after your crowned tell your mother you aren't going to marry and are going to be with all three of us. We can keep it a secret so as not to scandalize the country. We can be your personal guards."

Beck shook his head. "What about an heir?"

Addi spoke up. "The law doesn't say I have to be married for the heir to be legitimate. It's twenty-nineteen for god's sake, will it be such a big deal?"

Dorin shook his head. "This is crazy. We are one of the most traditional, stuck in the dark ages countries and you want to single-handedly make us the most progressive country in the world. This might kill your mother."

Addi smiled mischievously. "Actually, I have an idea about how to deal with her and get her to turn the crown over to me faster." She paced the room. "The bad news is, we have less than 30 hours to put my plan into action."

She walked over to her bedroom door and opened it. Shawna practically fell against her. "We're going to need your help too, come in."

Twenty

Addi stood in front of the mirror, she couldn't stop touching her ball gown. This was definitely a perk of being the Princess. She loved the whole spectacle of hair, makeup, and a gorgeous dress. That this particular event is in honor of her birthday only made it that more exciting.

Shawna grabbed the tiara from the mahogany box it was lying in and carefully set it on her head. The diamonds and pearls sparkled against her auburn curls. "You look beautiful, they are going to fall over themselves when they see you."

She twirled a few times looking at herself from all angles. The top of her dress was a sheer material the same color as her skin. Diamonds and pearls were sewn into the fabric to cover her chest and stomach. The jewels flowed down into a royal purple billowing satin skirt.

Addi couldn't help smiling as she caught sight of her back. Once she decided she was going to rebuke all customs and bring their palace into the twenty-first century, she contacted the designer and told them to leave her back completely open and not to get too heavy-handed in the front. Her mother was going to be pissed to see so much skin showing, but Addi was an adult now and eventually the Queen, so she was feeling confident enough to take small steps toward rebellion.

A soft knock on the door had them both turning. Mrs. Parsons walked in and stopped dead in her tracks. "Well, that is quite a dress, isn't it?"

Shawna beamed at her. "I think it is stunning."

Mrs. Parsons ignored her. "Everyone is in place, it's time for your grand entrance."

Nerves jumped in Addi's stomach, now that she was about to walk in front of a couple of hundred people she was suddenly regretting her wardrobe choice. Shawna leaned in and whispered to her. "You've slept with three guys this week, you are a badass, own it and show them who's Queen."

Addi gave her best friend a hug then held her chin high as she made her way to the ballroom. She could hear the roar of the crowd long before she got to the doors. Two servants opened the door for her, she stepped forward and looked down into the room. Every eye turned towards her, it had gone silent.

A wave of nausea hit her until she glanced down and found Dorin, Beck, and Noah standing at the bottom of the stairs waiting for her. She waited while she was announced then started descending the steps. She couldn't take her eyes off of her men. They were mouth-watering in their tuxedos, and the lust was evident in their eyes. Shawna was right, they loved the dress.

As she stepped in front of them, all three bowed deeply. Dorin reached for her hand and kissed the top of it. "My god, you are a vision, no longer our little ducky. You are definitely a swan."

Beck kissed her hand next. "You take my breath away."

Noah kissed her hand last. "The stars are surely dull tonight as your beauty outshines them all."

Addi blushed and thanked them. "Should we find my mother? I've managed to avoid her for the last day and a half, so I'm sure she's seething by now."

The foursome turned and made their way to the dais. Queen Ellena sat on an ornate chair and greeted guests as they were brought to her. The line stopped as Addi approached, she squared her shoulders and stared her mother straight in the eyes.

The Queen slowly took in Addi's dress from head to toe. "Did we get a new designer I'm unaware of?"

"Not at all, I called in a few changes that's all." Addi could see the anger in her eyes, but she was too polished to let it show.

Her mother glanced at each guy for a brief second. "I see you have all three with you. Are you sure you want to publicly declare your choice in front of the other two? Normally they are sent away before now."

Addi glanced around. "I can't make the announcement yet, I'm waiting on a special guest."

Dorin waved to someone off to the side. A man in his early forties was brought onto the dais. His suit was simple, he definitely didn't fit in with the rest of the people in the room. Addi was surprised how handsome he was. She could see why her mother would have fallen for him. He stopped in front of the Queen and bowed deeply. "It's good to see you again, Your Majesty."

Addi smiled, her mother was speechless. It was rare to see her caught off guard. She was definitely struggling for composure. "I need a moment." She stood and walked through a door behind her.

Dorin chuckled. "Well, that's not what I expected."

Addi started for the door. "Give me a moment with her."

She followed her mom to the private salon, she found her staring out a window. "Is it really him?"

Addi stopped a few feet away from her. "Yes, we found him."

Her mother turned. Addi was shocked to see tears rolling down her face. "How did you find him after all this time? Why did you find him?"

"It was a group effort; the guys enlisted the help of their families. He was a stable master at a manor across the border."

Addi was dying to know if her mom was happy to have her long lost love back or if they had made a terrible mistake.

Her mother wiped a tear from her chin. "What was your goal?"

"I wanted to remind you what love was, that it was worth fighting for. Your father wouldn't let you have your happily ever after. I'm begging you to let me have mine. Please don't make me choose between being the Queen and being with them. You won't like my choice."

The Queen stared at her, she could see the wheels turning but didn't know what she was thinking. She could feel they were on a precipice and needed to be pushed more.

Addi rushed back to the door, cracked it open and waved to the group. The older man stood hesitantly at the entrance. "Nathan, my name is Addilyn. It's nice to meet you. Would you like a few minutes with Ellena?"

He wiped his hands nervously on his pants. "I would, but that is her decision."

Addi turned and gave her mother a questioning look.

"Yes, of course."

Nathan walked in as Addi left the room and closed the door behind her. She leaned against the wall and let out a deep breath. All three guys were staring at her intently.

Dorin broke first. "Well?"

"She was crying, I've never actually seen her do that before. I think she's happy but also really confused."

Noah let out a deep breath. "Do you think it worked? Will she let you skip the announcement?"

The door creaked open, Nathan popped his head out. "She'd like to speak with all of you."

The fierce foursome clasped hands and walked in together, prepared to stand united.

Addi studied her mother's face, she was still crying, but she did seem happier.

Nathan walked back over and stood next to her. She smiled at him before turning back to Addi. "You played a risky game tonight. While I definitely don't approve of this." She waved her hands towards the four of them holding hands. "I won't make you choose anyone tonight. Go enjoy your birthday party, and if it's okay with you, I'm going to stay here and catch up with Nathan."

Her mother was actually asking how she felt about something? Who was this woman? "Yes, of course. I'll have cake and tea sent back later."

Before their good fortune could change, they left the room quickly. The war wasn't over, but at least this battle had been won.

Twenty-One

Addi's feet were killing her, she had danced all night long. She took her obligatory turns with visiting royals but most of her time was spent in the arms of one of her men. There were curious stares, Addi didn't pay them any mind.

She yawned discreetly behind her hand.

Dorin laughed. "I saw that. It's your party you know, you can leave when you want to."

Noah agreed. "I would love any excuse to leave, my face is going to break if I have to smile any longer."

Beck rolled his eyes at Noah. "We better get him out of here. We can't have anything happening to that pretty face of his."

They made their way around the room, avoiding as many people as possible until they made it to the side entrance that led to the servant's stairs. Addi immediately kicked her shoes off then made her way up to their floor.

The group stopped in front of her bedroom door. Addi held it open. "If you aren't too tired, I think we should discuss what's going to happen next."

All three nodded then followed her into her room. "I love this dress, but I am done. I need to change before we go any further."

She went to the bathroom and carefully undid the zipper at her waist and slid the dress off. She took off everything underneath and sighed with relief. A quick wash had her makeup off, she left the tiara on and grabbed her robe.

She walked out and found Dorin and Beck sitting on two of the chairs in the corner and Noah sitting on the edge of the bed, leaving the last chair for her.

She sat down and let the robe fall open enough to show a good portion of her legs. "I'm going to be honest with you. I love all three of you, and I want all three of you. I know it's unorthodox, but if you are willing to live together, I think we could make this relationship work."

The three guys exchanged glances. Beck cleared his throat. "So, to be clear. You aren't choosing one of us, you are keeping all of us?"

She smiled and nodded. "That's the plan."

Dorin held his hand up. "And how is that going to work?"

She stood and paced the room. "Well, I was thinking of a few options. It sounds really boring, but we could set up a schedule, and you each take a turn sleeping in here with me. Or we could have a larger bed brought in, and we could all sleep in here. You will still have your separate rooms for when you need time alone."

When she stopped and turned to them, her hands on her hips, proud of her ideas, she was surprised to see them all staring at her like she'd lost her mind.

Noah stood up. "I thought you were kidding when you were talking about running away and living together, but you are serious and about doing it here in the castle?"

Beck shook his head. "There is absolutely no way your mother is going to agree to this."

Addi shrugged. "I'm hoping Nathan keeps her so busy in the bedroom she doesn't notice and like we said earlier when I'm Queen I'm changing the rules. My children will not be forced into this ridiculous situation." All three heads snapped up to her. "Yes, children, I think I'd like at least one with each of you. That won't be a problem, will it?"

Dorin stood and took over pacing. "Addi, this is a lot. How will we know if it will even work?"

Addi walked over to the bed and smiled at them before untying her robe and sliding it off. She stood in all her naked glory. "I guess we're going to find out. You said you were trained to please me in all aspects of life. Right now, I want to be pleased by all three of you."

She climbed to the center of the bed and laid down.

For a few seconds, the guys stared at each other. She could see they were silently deciding what to do. Noah nodded, Beck shrugged, and Dorin smiled. All three turned and stripped as they walked towards the bed. Suddenly Addi was both turned on and apprehensive at the same time. She talked a big talk, but now she was actually going to do it, and she was intimidated at the idea.

Beck sat on her left, Dorin kneeled between her legs, and Noah walked around the bed to sit on her right. She hadn't been touched yet, but she was panting with nerves. It was erotic to have three men staring at her, waiting to devour her.

Noah leaned close. "I like the tiara, Princess." He kissed the side of her neck. "Is this what you wanted?"

Her eyes closed, she concentrated on the feeling of multiple hands running along her body. Their mouths seared her skin as they touched her. Dorin moved up her thighs until he reached her pussy. His tongue swirled circles around her already throbbing clit. Noah and Beck moved down until they each had a nipple in their mouths. The intensity of the moment was almost too much to bear. She squirmed, Dorin locked his arms around her thighs and held her hips still as he sucked on her.

She dug her hands into Noah and Beck's hair, she was close to combusting. The pressure built until she screamed out her orgasm.

Dorin's husky voice broke through her fog. "Did you enjoy that?"

"Mm-hmm."

Beck brushed the hair away that was clinging to her face. "Do you want more?"

She bit her lip, unsure what to do next. Instead, she simply nodded.

He laid down and rolled a condom on. "Straddle me, but I want you to face the end of the bed."

Addi swung her leg over, she lined his cock up and slid down. He gave her a second to adjust before pushing on her hips. She found a rhythm then gasped when Dorin pinched one nipple while his other hand reached down her ass. The shock of his finger stroking her hole had the intensity increasing. Unsure she could take more, she smiled when Noah stood on the bed in front of her. He grabbed her head and pulled it toward his dick. Greedy to experience more, she took him deep and sucked hard. The faster she rode Beck, and the deeper Dorin's finger went, the harder she sucked Noah. She didn't know long they went on like this, soon Noah was coming in her mouth. Shortly after she and Beck came too.

Addi slid to the side next to Beck and gasped for air. She had never experienced so many feelings at one time.

Dorin leaned over and kissed her lightly. "Happy Birthday, Princess."

She laughed. "Best birthday ever."

Epilogue

Two weeks later

Addi knocked quietly on her mother's door. They hadn't spoken much since the night of the ball. Addi had been spending time with the guys, and her mother had been catching up with Nathan.

Nathan opened the door. "Good Morning, Princess."

Addi tried to hide her surprise, she didn't realize they had gotten this close. "Good morning, Nathan and please call me Addi."

He stepped back and let her in. The Queen was sitting on her balcony, eating breakfast. Nathan started to walk out. "I'll give you two some time alone."

Addi took a deep breath and joined her mother. The first thing she noticed was how much younger she looked. The lines around eyes were smoother, she was smiling and genuinely seemed happy to see Addi. "Good morning, Dear."

Addi sat down, still shocked at the change. "Morning. I take it everything is good with Nathan? You aren't mad we brought him here?"

"It was shocking at first, I admit I had no idea what to do. Then we talked and got to know each other again. He's as sweet as he was back then." She turned to Addi. "And what about you? We have a lot to discuss, don't we?"

Addi wasn't sure what to say. Does she admit she's been sleeping with all of them, sometimes at the same time? She decided a simple nod was safer.

Ellena reached over and grabbed Addi's hand. "I've made a horrible mistake. I was blind and didn't see how my pain was being taken out on you, and I'm sorry for that. Now that Nathan is here again, I understand what you've been saying." She took a deep breath. "So, I'm not going to force you to choose one of them. If you marry, it will be for love, and you don't have to be married to take the crown from me, so that isn't an issue."

Tears burned Addi's eyes, her mother actually apologized to her. "Thank you for changing your mind. I really don't think I could have chosen."

Ellena sat back in her chair. "There is the question of what we're going to do about them though."

Addi rubbed her suddenly sweaty hands on her dress. "Well, about that, I'd like all of them to stay here as my personal guard. I can continue my relationship with them and from the outside people will be none the wiser."

Ellena's eyes widened. "Wait, are you saying you want to be with all three of them? I don't know that I can condone that."

It was Addi's turn to grab her mother's hand and plead with her. "It may not make sense to you, but we're meant to be together. I think we've always known it. You have to admit no one will ever love and protect me as much as those three will."

Ellena bit her lip as she contemplated what Addi was asking. "What about my grandchildren, will they all be illegitimate? Have you discussed this with the guys, will only one of them be fathering your children?"

Addi coughed, nervous to talk about such a personal topic with her when they had never spoken of these things before. "We're only eighteen, so we have time to work it out. I do hope to have children by all three of them. They deserve to be father's if they want to be." She shrugged as she sat back. "Plus, I checked, and there is nothing in our laws that says the heir has to be legitimate."

Ellena sighed. "You have thought this through, haven't you? If you agree to not flaunt your relationships in public, I will let this continue. We'll announce we're no longer following the old ways and children will no longer be chosen to live at the palace." She got up and paced the balcony. "We'll be strategic and have you and the guys as your guards spending time out in public, doing charity work. If you have the people on your side, they won't balk at the idea of you having a child."

Addi stood up and stopped her mother. "You're still willing to give me the crown even though I might cause a scandal?"

Ellena cupped Addi's cheeks. "I know I've not said this before, but the people already adore you. Let them see you care about the country, and they will respect you. I know you have other changes you want to make. Bring them into the future with you, and you will have their loyalty."

Addi couldn't remember the last time her mother hugged her, but she'll never forget this moment when she wrapped her in her arms and accepted her for who she was. She loved her enough to let her make her own royal choice.

The End

Want a bonus scene? Sign up for my newsletter and see where Addi and her boys are now!
https://dl.bookfunnel.com/tkk7oxoifc

ABOUT THE AUTHOR

Cassidy lives in the Tampa, Florida area with her high school sweetheart, their three children, two crazy dogs, a guinea pig and a skinny pig. She loves reading and going to the movies but not nearly as much as she enjoys watching her kids either playing ball or performing with one of their instruments. She also loves to travel and hopes to one day watch a baseball game in every MLB stadium in the country.

To learn more about Cassidy please visit her online at www.cassidykoconnor.com.

You can also find her on Facebook at www.facebook.com/cassidykoconnorauthor

She always welcomes new friends and encourages readers to reach out to her.

~Other Books by the Author~

<u>Raven's Haven Series</u>
Fighting For Forgiveness

Sassy Mates: In My Mate's Sight
Sassy Mates: In My Mate's Defense

Paranormal Dating Agency: My Oath To You

Broken Dreams

Forever Yours, Casey

The Laird's Promise

Sexy In White

To Steal a Prince's Heart

Wicked Wonderland Retreat Box Set

<u>The Love's Protector Series</u>
Awakening Her Desires
The Evolution of Sam
Finding His Swing

The Black Hollow Series

The town of Black Hollow has many more stories to tell. Please visit the website and join the Facebook group to know when the next story is releasing.

https://www.blackhollowtown.com/
https://www.facebook.com/blackhollowtown/

Books in the Black Hollow Series
(In order by Publication Date)

Loving the Monster Within (Prequel)

by Cassidy K. O'Connor

Reviving Love by Cassidy K. O'Connor

Silver Linings by Sheri Lyn

Finding Her Fire by Gracen Miller

One Man's Curse by Jennifer Wedmore

It's the Little Things by Robbie Cox

Resurrecting His Heart by J.C. Layne

Sacrificing Love by Cassidy K. O'Connor